Lifelines

Lifelines

New Writing from Bangladesh

Edited by
FARAH GHUZNAVI

zubaan

ZUBAAN
an imprint of Kali for Women
128B Shahpur Jat
1st floor
New Delhi 110 049
Email: contact@zubaanbooks.com
www.zubaanbooks.com

First published by Zubaan, 2012

Copyright © Farah Ghuznavi, 2012
Copyright © individual stories with the authors, 2012

All rights reserved*

10 9 8 7 6 5 4 3 2 1

ISBN: 978 93 81017 84 5

Zubaan is an independent feminist publishing house based in New Delhi, India, with a strong academic and general list. It was set up as an imprint of the well known feminist house Kali for Women and carries forward Kali's tradition of publishing world quality books to high editiorial and production standards. 'Zubaan' means tongue, voice, language, speech in Hindustani. Zubaan is a non-profit publisher, working in the areas of the humanities and social sciences, as well as in fiction, general non-fiction, and books for young adults that celebrate difference, diversity and equality, especially for and about the children of India and South Asia under its imprint Young Zubaan.

Typeset in Meridien LT Std 10/14 by Jojy Philip, New Delhi 110 015
Printed at Raj Press, R-3 Inderpuri, New Delhi 110 012

Contents

Acknowledgements

It is a matter of considerable pride for me to have had this opportunity to help bring English writing from Bangladesh to the attention of a wider audience. And I have learned a tremendous amount along the way. Things that will help me to improve my own writing; and a variety of virtues—primary among them patience and persistence—that should help remedy the shortcomings in my character!

There are a number of people whom I must thank for their contributions and support during the process of putting together this collection:

The contributors who trusted me with their stories and patiently bore the ordeal of having their darlings disciplined (though I steadfastly claim that no stories were killed in the process of creating this anthology)

Urvashi Butalia and Preeti Gill for their faith in this book and in Bangladeshi writers—and for their determination that I should be the one to edit the collection even though it was nearly two years before I finally succumbed to the temptation of doing so myself

Mahmud Rahman, Lena Hasle, Tove Kittelsen and Jan Pihl for their unflagging encouragement and brainstorming/technical services; Shabnam Nadiya for introducing me to the work of Tayeba Begum Lipi, who kindly allowed us use her painting 'Gothna on Venus' for the cover of *Lifeline*, and Aasha Amin, Lori Simpson, Sharbari Ahmed, Sadat Saaz Siddiqi, Saad Z. Hossain, Sigrid Anna Oddsen, Faustina Pereira, Masud Khan Shujon, M.K. Aaref, Awrup Sanyal, Abeer Hoque, and Kazi Anis Ahmed for moral support

All those who have actively encouraged me to write, from Professor Niaz Zaman, Sara Zaker and my various writer communit(ies), to my loyal 'first readers' Sian Ghuznavi, Adiba Rahman and Trimita Chakma. Every writer should have such a support structure!

And last, but so very much not least, my parents Farhad and Ruby Ghuznavi, whom I owe more than I can ever articulate or repay, for their unflinching faith in my capacities—which so far outstrips my own—and their singular willingness to support me in whatever hare-brained endeavours I have undertaken to date

Introduction

When Zubaan first approached me nearly three years ago to edit this anthology, I was both thrilled and apprehensive. The idea of having a collection of new writing from Bangladesh on Indian and international bookshelves was immensely appealing. The time commitment it involved—especially the time taken away from my own writing—was rather less so. The problem for me was that I wanted to contribute to the anthology, not to actually be responsible for editing it! And I said as much.

The criteria Zubaan had in mind for this collection also posed challenges of a different kind. A newer generation of writers was to be featured, in their forties or younger; all the stories needed to have been originally written in English; and it would be an all-female cast of contributors. A year passed, and we were well into the second year after the initial discussion had taken place, periodically touching upon the possibility of bringing out this anthology whenever I met with friends and colleagues at Zubaan, before I realised that I had to put aside my reservations and just do it. So I did.

The experience has been unforgettable. After selecting and editing these fifteen stories, I find that I have learned more than I ever expected to, and not just about what it means to have the not insignificant responsibilities of an editor. Through the process of identifying and negotiating substantive changes in the stories with fourteen very different fellow contributors, I have learned patience, humility, persistence—and perhaps most importantly, quite a bit about what constitutes good writing and how one might actually become a better writer. And since becoming a better writer is something that I dream of and work at on an almost daily basis, that means a great deal.

Writers in Bangladesh have always taken pride in their literary heritage, and with good reason. While much of Bengali literature, in the form of novels, plays, poetry and short stories, remains inaccessible due to the lack of high-quality translations, there is a wealth of written material that lies waiting to be discovered by the wider world. This considerable body of work also draws on earlier oral traditions, and reflects variations in regional dialects.

Women writers have long had an established place within the pantheon of writers from Bengal, including those from Bangladesh. The work of novelists and poets such as Sufia Kamal, Mahasweta Devi, Razia Khan Amin, Selina Hossain, Shaheen Akhter and other contemporary authors—as well as the pioneering work of Rokeya Sakhawat Hossain before them—outstanding as it is, remains only partially accessible to a wider audience. It has been suggested that the reason Rokeya Sakhawat Hossain chose to write her seminal work *Sultana's Dream* in English (she later translated it into Bengali herself) was in order to make the thoughts and ideas of Bengali women accessible to a larger readership. And as Selina Hossain noted at the Hay Festival Dhaka in 2011, this remains a challenge for many of those writing in Bengali.

More recently however, socioeconomic changes within the country and the widespread impact of globalisation have helped to shape the development of a newer generation of voices from Bangladesh. Many of these women writers choose to express themselves in English, and their life experiences, as well as their understanding of their Bangladeshi identity, vary enormously. As is to be expected, these variations are reflected in their work. Only a handful of such writers, including Monica Ali and Tahmima Anam, have received significant attention on the world stage so far, but their numbers are likely to rise in the near future given the works-in-progress that are approaching completion. And although putting pen to paper remains in many ways an act of defiance and a statement of nonconformity—and despite a continuous battle with self-censorship—some of them are choosing to challenge and redefine what women supposedly should or shouldn't write about.

This is a generation that has seen travel and overseas educations become the norm for those who can afford it; a generation where attitudes to sex and drug use are very different from those that existed even a few decades ago. Living and working abroad for a few years is not as unusual as it once was, and many have done so—from highly-paid professionals to the migrant labourers who contribute so much to the Bangladeshi economy with their remittances.

Unsurprisingly, work by the writers in this volume reflects a noticeable urban bias, whether their stories are set in the Bangladeshi capital Dhaka, or in cities around the globe, like New York, Nairobi, Addis Ababa, London or Vancouver. But some have also chosen more traditional settings, including villages, *mofussil* towns and provincial university campuses.

It is not only the emergence of a "global Bangladeshi" identity that is reflected in such new writing. In the last four decades, the work of non-government organisations such as BRAC and Grameen Bank, along with many others, has drastically changed attitudes and expectations in much of the countryside. Ideas about women's education, employment prospects and romantic relationships are among the most affected, despite the persistence of gender discrimination and violence.

In many ways this has been a gradual evolution, but it has broken down the urban-rural divide in ways that were unimaginable a generation ago. The opening up of jobs for single women from rural areas in the urban-centred garment industry is just one of the factors that have contributed to change. This is a country where tertiary education for women, though limited, is higher than ever before; and industrial employment opportunities have become not only a recognisable part of the social fabric, but something that many women aspire to.

The outreach of cable TV to the countryside, and the popularity of Bollywood (and closer to home, Dhallywood) have helped to shape cultural expectations of romance, while the widespread use of mobile telephone technology has revolutionised communications. And in an era where, for example, pornography applications in Bengali—in the form of both visuals and text—are easily accessible on the mobile phone network, the changes in social attitudes that these factors have combined to bring about are not limited to a single social class.

In cities like the capital Dhaka, the particularities of the urban lifestyle in its various forms, and the sense of being connected to and affected by a wider world and its trends, are almost palpable. It is this Bangladesh—in all its diversity, contradictions, beauty, chaos, extremes and confusion—that makes its appearance in this new collection of women's writing. And that is part of what carries these stories beyond the more conventional boundaries of what are considered "women's themes", into territory that is harder to categorise.

Selecting a title for this collection was a challenge—the sheer diversity of the tales showcased here meant that a single overarching theme was nigh-impossible to identify. The protagonists and points of view featured in these stories include both women and men, in different stages of life, from varied backgrounds, living in urban and rural settings that range from villages and provincial towns to cities and mega-cities.

I chose "Lifelines" as the anthology title because it reflects a number of key themes. Most of the characters in these pages are making journeys of their own—physical and/or psychological—to reach resolutions that are often unexpected, if not always unwelcome. In the process, they are learning to adapt to situations that are beyond what they have previously experienced—and transforming themselves in ways which they never anticipated.

In palmistry, the life line predicts the fate of an individual: the path their life will take, how long they will be around to live it. For others, life lines are those marks, visible or unseen, that their experiences leave on the face, the body and soul. For the protagonists of these stories, lifelines are also what they need when they find themselves in unanticipated crises. And as they navigate their way through these situations—sometimes serendipitously, sometimes painfully—they each end up crafting their own destiny, one that is a 'work in progress'.

We read about events taking place at different stages in the characters' life cycles. A number of contributors have chosen childhood as their setting, allowing for the use of a very particular viewpoint—and a degree of clarity about situations that is sometimes harder for adults to acknowledge or capture. Sharbari Ahmed's "Pepsi" tells the story of a child whose privileged status as the offspring of UN workers in Addis Ababa cannot compensate her for the loneliness of their peripatetic lifestyle; when the opportunity for companionship comes from an unexpected source, she takes it without thought for the consequences. Shabnam Nadiya's "Teacher Shortage" provides a chilling insight into how the adults in a provincial university campus community refuse to acknowledge the spousal abuse taking place behind closed doors, which is an open secret among the children who play together. Tisa Muhaddes' story "Over and Over Again" examines another form of gender violence, where the actions of a paedophile uncle have unimaginable consequences for everyone caught up in the situation.

Sexual awakening and the confusion it often brings in its wake are touched upon in several of the stories. In "Gandaria", Iffat Nawaz describes a young girl's growing awareness of sexual undercurrents within her wider family. Rubaiyat Khan's "Rida" demonstrates how protestations of love can intermingle with the violence of sexual obsession. Abeer Hoque's "Wax Doll" portrays a young woman trying to identify the decision that will bring her happiness, caught between the desires she doesn't fully understand, and the illusion of security offered by an arranged marriage.

Romance and desire are recurrent themes, whether from the viewpoint of an older man seeking his lost love in Munize Manzur's "Bookends", or the young woman in Lori S. Khan's "Mehendi Dreams" who tries to understand—at her younger sister's henna ceremony—why she herself should be considered so much less desirable. These emotions also underlie some of the stories that may be considered more traditional in content, such as Shazia Omar's portrayal of the tensions between a mother-in-law and her daughter-in-law in "Table for Three" or Sadaf Saaz Siddiqui's age-old tale of seduction, pregnancy and rejection "Daydreams". But neither of the stories is quite what it seems at first glance;the twist in the tale relates to the real cause of the tension between the two women in the first story, and the far from traditional way in which the final outcome is decided in the second.

As might be expected in a contemporary anthology from Bangladesh, migration in its many guises is a key theme. Studying abroad is one such experience, and—in these stories—does not necessarily evoke a sense of displacement for the protagonist, though memories of the past are inevitably transported along with the traveller. In S. Bari's "Touch Me Not", a young man travels to America, only to find himself catapulted back to a rural childhood by an unexpected encounter with someone from his past. Similarly, Sabrina Ahmad's "Something Fishy" shows how a postgraduate student discovers, after receiving a fishy gift, that echoes of Bangladesh have followed her all the way to Canada.

For others, migration offers a form of escape, though things may not always turn out as expected— and revisiting the past may reveal that events were not always quite as they might have seemed. In Srabonti Narmeen Ali's "Yellow

Cab", the narrator realises the limits of opportunity as he reflects on his failed aspirations and his fall from grace after the events of 9/11. In my own story, "Getting There", a successful female architect is forced to return to the port city of Chittagong—a place of bitter childhood memories—after a family accident forces her to face up to what she rejected years ago by moving to Dhaka. The story placed second in a competition at Oxford, and was commended for tackling the consequences of a changing society "with great ability, variety and clarity".

In all these stories, characters develop their unique and sometimes surprising strategies to deal with what life has handed out to them. For some, silence is a defence mechanism; for others a weapon, or a form of resistance. Displacement is by no means specific to those who have moved elsewhere—it lives within troubled souls who must chart their own paths to peace of a kind, developing maps for journeys even as they are travelling them. Help to overcome adverse circumstances can come from unexpected quarters: technology such as the Internet or DNA testing, or even the catchy music of Chubby Checker. But most of all, as Alizeh Ahmed's short piece "Be" illustrates, it lies within—the individual's untapped ability to fashion a lifeline in order to escape the vagaries of life and circumstance.

For me, this anthology has been a labour of love, with the stress on both 'labour' and 'love'. In the process of putting it together, I have encountered deadlines which appeared impossible to meet, and obstacles that sometimes seemed insuperable given the time and resource constraints involved. I have been fortunate to have had helping hands offered on more than one occasion. And I have shared first-hand these characters' experiences of fashioning lifelines out of thin air. At the end of it all, I remain immensely glad to have had the experience of working on this book, and I can only hope that readers will be as pleased with the final volume that they hold in their hands.

Teacher Shortage

What happened in Mitul's house was the best-kept secret in our campus town. Usually—ours being a small community, and one that took neighbourliness to wicked extremes—everyone knew what was cooking in everyone else's pot. When the whole thing finally came out, it absolutely astonished the campus aunties how they could not have known what was going on. Or so they said.

We had known, of course; kids always do. Mitul told Pamela and me about her father. We knew her grandparents lived with them, and Pamela asked the obvious: 'Don't they say anything to your father? Don't they stop him?'

Mitul looked steadily at the mangled blade of grass she held in her hand; she had been chewing it for some time. 'My *Dada* sometimes hits my *Dadi* as well.'

If we had been older, perhaps we would have understood it better. We would have known enough to think that Sharif Uncle, Mitul's father, was maybe copying behaviour that had been imprinted on his brain; he must have witnessed

An earlier version of this story appeared in *New Age Eid Special* (Bangladesh) 2008.

his father bashing his mother's brains out since babyhood. We might have wondered why Mitul's mother took it, why she didn't just leave. But then, if we had been old enough, we would have known: women in her situation rarely do.

Mitul would often report the goings-on at her house to us. We listened to Mitul's revelations with a mingling of surprise and bewilderment. Usually, she would vouchsafe these incidents when the three of us were alone in one of our favourite places: the dam, the concrete jetty by the lake, the broad tree-shaded field between the Library Building and the Ladies Hall. She would deliver her news in a matter-of-fact voice, almost in a monotone. As if the triteness of the violence occurring in her home every other day had robbed her of the minimum interest needed to add colour and tone. We were too young then to comprehend the truly mundane quality of her recital—her mother was just another wife to have been slammed against a bedroom wall, to have a chair pushed into her ribs, an iron or a bowl of hot *dal* thrown at her face. The boring everydayness of the reasons that Mitul reported with such journalistic fervour only puzzled us further, and left me mute; the *dal* often lacked salt in our house as well, and sometimes the beds remained unmade even after breakfast was over and done with.

Mitul's *Dada* had once slapped Putul in front of her. This didn't seem too bad to us—we received slaps on a more or less regular basis from our parents anyway. But it did jar. In our experience, grandparents never disciplined you, not ever. And the younger ones, the babies of the family, were especially precious to the old people. I shied away from asking too many questions. But Pamela was always curious about everything. Why did he slap Putul? She must've done something *really* bad to make their grandfather slap her. The reply, that she had done nothing, not really, she had just left her books lying around after finishing her homework, made no sense to us.

We were too young still to have learnt that it was in the nature of campus secrets that everyone knew. Ignorance was *not* why a secret was a secret. I remember Pamela's mother and their next-door aunty exchanging swift glances when Pamela blurted out Mitul's secret. I pinched Pamela's upper arm, but as usual where Pamela and her big mouth were concerned, it was too late. Her mother took a careful sip of tea and asked softly, 'Where did you hear *that,* dear? I'm sure it's not true.'

There was a sweetish tang to the air we inhaled, as if decaying roses were bunched somewhere just out of sight. My fingertips tingled, yet Pamela went on: 'She told us, *Ammu*! Mitul told us.'

'Oh really,' her mother tinkled. 'I'm sure you misheard her.'

'But she did,' insisted Pamela desperately. 'You were there, you tell them,' Pamela turned to me. 'She did say so.'

I looked at the lace border of the tray cloth on which the gold-trimmed cups rested. It was no use, I knew. Why Pamela couldn't figure it out I didn't know. I waited silently, trying to follow the intricate mesh of white cotton thread, as if unravelling it with my eyes. I knew it was crocheted lace, I had seen my grandma crochet. I imagined a pair of blue-veined old hands busy, busy, busy, with a sharp needle pushing and pulling its way through this white stuff.

I heard the other aunty say in her sharp voice, 'Mitul was joking, Pamela. Maybe she was angry at her father for punishing her for something. And I don't wonder—making up such stories! Such things don't happen *here*, for goodness sake.'

Pamela obstinately opened her mouth again, her fat lips parting like those of a blowfish ready to gulp some more air. I pulled at her arm. 'Come on,' I said insistently. 'You said you would show me your new dress. Come on.' Pamela was my best friend, she was, but sometimes I could just kill her.

· ·◦◦◦· · ◦◦◦· ·

Then Mitul's mother became our geography teacher. Mitul told us that they had been visited by three of the uncles who sat on the school committee. They had said that Mitul's mother was being wasted sitting at home with her M.Sc. degree. Her father was none too happy about it, but for the moment the school's need seemed to be greater than his.

I had heard my father grumbling about how they were ruining the school through short-term policies. Apparently, the housing shortage had led the university authorities to encourage the school to employ the wives of teachers or officers. That way they wouldn't have to provide the schoolteachers with separate accommodation, as they were already living on campus.

My parents were worried that the housing shortage was receiving higher priority than the qualified teacher shortage. They weren't certain that anyone was making sure that the wives who were being engaged were good teachers. But I didn't care. Sharif Aunty was nice and she was a good teacher. Some kids made snide remarks about Mitul having her own Ma teaching her class, but we ignored them.

And then one summer's day, Mitul's mother turned up at the campus health centre with a sprained wrist. She said she had slipped and fallen in the bathroom, but the banged-up wrist was accompanied by a blackish bruise almost the same shape as an iron. Sister Onima of the eagle eye spotted the upside-down iron shape on Sharif Aunty's lower back as she was winding a crepe bandage around her wrist. Sharif Aunty had pulled the *anchal* of her sari around herself, covering herself from curious eyes, but the flimsy material of the sari had not concealed her secret for too long.

Sister Onima came to visit my mother in the late afternoon. I was at the dining table having my afternoon snack. 'It's disgraceful,' I heard her say. 'Absolutely indecent. Someone should put a stop to it.' My mother wound the corner of her sari *anchal* around her finger as she listened.

It took me almost an hour to finish my glass of milk that day. As I nibbled at a forkful of noodles as slowly as I dared, I heard my mother say in a tight little voice, 'Well, I don't know. I know that *I* wouldn't stand for it. The first time he raises his hand to me, it's bye-bye mister sahib. I'll just pack my bags, take my child, and leave for my father's house. There's a limit to everything.' Sister Onima had a cup of tea and left, sighing.

That evening my mother was tight-lipped and her eyes had a curiously cold shine to them, as if the water in there was gradually turning into ice. 'Have you heard?' she asked as soon as my father walked into the house.

'Err, what?' he replied cautiously. He knew her moods; he could tell at a glance that she was bare moments away from a full-blown explosion.

'Well, Mrs Sharif's an employee of the school now. You're on the committee. Aren't you going to do anything about this? We all know what happens in that house. It's been going on long enough,' she said.

An uncomfortable silence reigned between them. My father was mostly a mild-mannered man, rarely roused to anger. I couldn't remember the last time he had raised his hand to me, and if my mother and he had their occasional squabbles, they never seemed any more serious than the spats I would have with Pamela. I was still at the dining table. This time it was my homework I was lingering over, awaiting the blessed relief of dinnertime.

Ma would light into my father occasionally on his various shortcomings, and I could always tell when he was halfway between being scared of her and angry at her. A muscle just above his left cheekbone would twitch. From there it could go either way. On this occasion, he pressed down for a while on the twitching muscle in his cheek.

In a low voice, hoping perhaps that it would escape my eager ears while at the same time deflecting Ma from the warpath, he said, 'It's so easy to judge from the outside, isn't it? I mean, do we really know what goes on in that house? I mean, it's between the husband and the wife, right? What business do we have there?'

My mother sat speechless, her lower lip hanging open for a few seconds until she suddenly snapped it shut. I knew that speechlessness of hers well. I was often at the receiving end of it, due to unsatisfactory report cards, appearance, and behaviour. I also knew that this state of hers never lasted too long.

'That woman,' she enunciated slowly as if speaking to the wizened old beggar woman who came every week and who would only smile and nod at whatever was said to her, 'is *abused*.'

He sighed. 'Look, she hasn't made any complaints, has she?'

'What has that got to do with anything? And what about the children?'

My father sighed again, and remained quiet. The chair he sat in creaked as if trying to fill the silence. I had my head down almost flat against the tabletop, furiously outlining random numbers in a semblance of the problems set out in my book. He must have gestured towards me or something, for I heard my mother's ice-voice call to me. 'Why don't you go upstairs and watch some television?'

Television before dinnertime? This was unprecedented in our house. I looked up to say something to her, but thought better of it. I began to tidy up my school stuff as the smell of frying fish wafted in from the kitchen. I climbed the stairs to the accompaniment of the low, excited voices of my parents punctuated by the crackle and sizzle of spiced fish being dropped into hot oil.

The next morning, there were the usual *ruti*, potato *bhaji* and omelette at the breakfast table and the usual class with Sharif Aunty at school. My parents went out that evening to attend a dinner party at the house of one of the new arrivals.

It wasn't too long after that evening that Mitul's grandmother died. I remember going with my mother to their house, after the maid from next door delivered the news. They had just brought the dead body back from the useless trip to the hospital.

The old lady we used to steal pickles from had been laid out on the verandah for mourners to pay their last respects.

She would be taken away to her husband's ancestral village for burial, which was three or four hours' journey by bus from our campus.

When we reached the house, we found that her face was covered. I felt curiosity. This was not the first dead body I had seen, but it was the first old one. The fabric that lay beside the body dazzled me with its whiteness. It shone as eager hands unfolded it and held it spread out over Mitul's *Dadi*, as if they were trying to shelter her from the morning sun. My mother had covered her head with her sari, like all the other women present. She walked towards them and asked, 'Has she been bathed yet?'

'Oh, don't even ask.' Pamela's mother flung out her hands in exasperation. She was standing to one side, glaring at Mitul's grandmother's dead body, the white cloth, the people filing past the body in quick succession. 'What are we supposed to do with the *murda* once we bathe her? The cloth they've brought isn't enough to cover her. What irresponsible...'

Mitul's next-door Aunty broke in firmly, 'We don't know that yet, *Bhabi*, do we?' She turned to my mother and said, 'That's why we've unfolded it, you know. We're trying to figure out if this will do, or whether we have to send someone to get a new shroud.'

My mother moved nearer as the other aunties began commenting, commending, and protesting, and it seemed as if their voices all merged into a deepening chant—holy yet unsatisfying.

It was only later, when I went and stood beside Mitul and Putul who were sitting together, weeping silently, that sorrow overwhelmed the distant curiosity I felt. 'They're taking the *murda* away,' the murmur reached the second floor and passed me by. 'Bring the women down, they're taking her away.'

'*Bhabi,*' someone called to Sharif Aunty who sat silently in a straight-backed chair in the master bedroom. 'Come down for the last look, they'll take her away now.'

Neither the two sisters nor their mother were to accompany the old woman on her journey; the presence of women in a graveyard was frowned upon. Mitul's father and grandfather would ease her into her final resting place, as was fitting.

Hitherto silent, Sharif Aunty took one look at her mother-in-law's face and began screaming, 'Oh *Amma, Amma,* how can I live here now? Who will look after me? Who will look after me? Oh *Amma,* don't leave me, oh *Amma*...' She flopped down, her limbs askew like those rag dolls my grandmother had made for me when I was younger. The aunties surrounding her caught her and held her up, and somehow she was gradually borne back to the house.

The sickening, sweetish smell of the slow-burning *agarbatti* filled the air. It fused with the sounds of the *Kalimah Shahadat* as myriad voices called out '*Ashhadu alla ilaha illallahu*...'

The dead body, bathed and wrapped in the shroud, was covered with a bed sheet and Mitul's father and uncles hoisted the cheap wooden *khatia* onto their shoulders. They carried the *khatia* to the truck waiting outside, and got into the back with it. Other men squeezed in. Mitul's grandfather got in at the front. Some of them began drifting back to their regular haunts. The women would remain for a while.

'Well, I've never seen anyone cry like that for a mother-in-law!' Pamela's mother's wonderment could easily have been appeased by me. But I remained silent, standing by my mother's side. Thankfully, Pamela was nowhere to be seen.

Mitul rarely came to sit with Pamela and me after her *Dadi* died. We didn't really notice. Mitul had also begun missing classes. That too went unnoticed. Sharif Aunty was taking the classes she was supposed to, but she went around in a kind of daze, unseeing, unhearing. Her full-sleeved blouses seemed odd in summer, but who would ask her about it? It was no one's business what a woman chose to wear to her workplace.

We were dawdling by the side of the road one day when we spied Putul coming towards us. Three years younger than we were, in the past she had tried desperately to hang out with us, but Mitul never allowed her sister to tag along. The past year or so, Putul had stopped dogging our footsteps. Another thing we hadn't noticed.

When we saw her, we went back to our old trick of teasing her:

> Mitul Putul Mitul Putul
> Putul is a huge futul
> Futul means big bang
> Putul has no gang!

Neither of us had any idea what on earth that was supposed to mean, but reciting it at the top of our voices five or six times always had the satisfactory effect of making Putul cry and run off home, so that she stopped pestering us. But not that day.

Pamela and I shouted our litany at the top of our voices, but we faltered once or twice. Perhaps it was because that nonsense rhyme was used to having three voices ringing out in a chorus, so that the rhythm wavered, unbalanced by our unfamiliar duet. Instead of breaking down in tears, Putul moved inexorably towards us. She dropped her schoolbag on the ground. As she came to a stop in front of us, we finally shut up, cowed by the solemn determination in the little girl's face.

'Why do you always do that to me?' she asked in her quiet manner.

'We... It's just a rhyme.' I answered lamely.

'But you make me cry,' she said. She paused and repeated, 'You always make me cry.'

I had no answer to that, but Pamela piped up, 'Well, your sister does it too. Why don't you go yell at her?'

Putul looked at Pamela for a while, then began walking away. I called her back. 'Putli, listen.' She stopped and turned towards us, but stood where she was, not venturing any nearer. I walked to her and tried to take her hand. She was stiff, but she let me. I held her hand; she did not hold mine.

'Putul, why doesn't Mitul come to play with us anymore? She hasn't come in ages.'

Putul looked at me steadily as she replied, 'She's your friend, why don't you go ask her?'

I could feel the anger within her make her tremble slightly, a muted quivering like the unheard hum of taut bowstrings or a just-strung sitar.

'Please don't be like that, Putul. Just tell me, is she angry with us?'

Pamela called to me from behind, 'There's no need to butter her up. If she doesn't want to talk, fine. Let's just go.'

But for some reason I couldn't leave. I held onto her hand

as if so much that was unsaid depended on it, and pleaded, 'I didn't realize, Putul, I'm sorry. I thought…'

Putul interrupted me, 'It's okay, *Apu*.' I felt her hand relax in mine. 'We just need to be home more now. Now that mother is alone.'

I didn't understand what she meant: why was her mother alone? Mothers were never alone—mothers were just, well, mothers.

She gripped my hand now, the calm sweat of her palm rubbing off onto mine. 'I'll tell Mitul *Apu* you asked about her.' She hesitated, then added, 'It's okay to visit our house, you know. You can come see Mitul *Apu*.'

I opened my mouth to tell her that we most certainly would, but I heard Pamela's voice grate in my ears. 'Well, yeah, but only when your father's not home, right?'

Putul stared at her for a while, then blinked at me once. She gently disengaged her hand, which I still held, and picked up her school bag. She walked away, holding her bag up with one hand and dusting it off with the other. I looked at the bit of earth where the bag had lain, noting the vibrant green of the grass, offset by slightly yellowing fallen leaves, a discoloured candy wrapper.

Pamela moved impatiently behind me and tugged at my arm. 'That little bitch! C'mon, let's go home.' We were supposed to go over to her house and paint our nails silver. Pamela's aunt who lived in the US had sent her six bottles of nail polish. Our mothers would have cheerfully killed us if we had asked either of them to buy us nail polish, but I guess since it was a gift from abroad it didn't really count as makeup and we weren't losing our little girlishness too soon if we used it.

Pamela put her arm around my waist, with her other arm behind her back, waiting for mine to conjoin and complete the twisted chain. We would occasionally skip this way, our bodies close together, in time, in rhythm. But this only worked for two friends; we never did it when Mitul was with us.

I shook my head and began walking homewards. I took little comfort from the look on Pamela's face, hurt and bewildered. Nail painting would have to wait for another day.

· ·◊◊◊· ·◊◊◊· ·

I was eating my breakfast as my mother sipped her tea, grumbling about how I got through school uniforms like a demon. Everyone else needed one set a year. Mine had to be replaced twice. It was Friday, and the weekend allowed me to dawdle over my food to the familiarly comfortable accompaniment of my mother's twice-yearly moaning. Father had almost finished his tea and was rustling through the newspaper. The doorbell rang. I heard Firoza, our maid, open the door.

There was some talk. I heard a woman's voice. Firoza came to Ma and said, 'It's Mitul's mother. She wants to see you, *Khalamma*.' There was something in her voice that made all of us look at her. 'She wants to see you.' Firoza repeated.

The cup clattered onto the saucer as Ma hurried to the door. I heard an 'Oh Allah!' There was silence for a few seconds and then, 'Come in, *Bhabi*, come in. Tell me what happened.'

Her head hanging low, Sharif Aunty walked in with my mother's arm encircling her. They were followed by Mitul

and Putul. I knew that the dresses they were wearing were
the ones they slept in. Mitul's dress was ripped under the
collar. Her mother didn't know about it, or she would have
darned it. Mitul used to stick her finger in the rip and worry
it on nights when she couldn't fall asleep.

Ma helped Sharif Aunty to a chair. She flopped down
into it with the unboned grace of a doll. When she raised her
head, I caught a quick glimpse of the purplish stain across the
right side of her face, like a map indicating the boundaries of
a separate country within a larger whole.

Father made a gurgling sound in his throat and stood up.
'*Bhabi*, have some tea, won't you? *Ei*, I'm leaving.' There
was a quick exchange of looks between my parents as my
father folded the newspaper and rushed out as if he were
late for class.

'This is too much. Something must be done about this.'
My mother touched the purple on Sharif Aunty's cheek and
repeated, 'This cannot go on.'

'No,' came the soft response. 'No, not anymore.' She was
silent for a moment, as our curiosity dangled in the air. 'I'm
leaving him.'

The enormity of her words took hold of my heart and
shook it. Ma heaved a sigh and began, 'Well, that *is* news!
And…'

'If you could just let us stay for a few days…' Sharif Aunty
cut into my mother's relief. The words sounded hollow, as if
emerging from cavernous depths. 'Just for a few days. I'm a
teacher at the school now. They'll give me my own quarters
for sure.'

My mother handed me my glass of milk, her movements
taut. She didn't look at Sharif Aunty as she buttered another

slice of bread. Mitul and Putul were sitting at our table looking at the plates Firoza had silently placed in front of them. They each held a duplicate of my own breakfast: an orange-yolked poached egg, two slices of toasted bread, a banana, and a slice of papaya. Ma slid the slice of bread she had buttered onto my plate. But although I had had only one slice, I no longer felt like breakfast.

'Why don't you take Mitul and Putul up to your room and play?' my mother suggested. I had never obeyed my mother as promptly as I did at that moment, pushing back my chair and standing up before she had even finished suggesting that we leave.

But Sharif Aunty's hard voice sucked the movement from my feet. 'What is it that you want to hide from them?' She looked at me and then at my mother. She smiled at her daughters.

'They know all there is to know. What is it that we can hide?'

But I knew what it was that my mother had wanted to hide. I knew from the tightly coiled strength of her skin. I knew from the way she gripped the butter knife, the slight silent rhythm of her foot tapping under the table, the way she had pulled her sari end around her to hide her shoulders. I knew that a few days weren't enough, that despite being a teacher Sharif Aunty would never be allotted living quarters, that Mitul and Putul would end up following their mother down whatever narrowing path they had left ahead of them.

'What about your brothers?' asked Ma.

Sharif Aunty's parents were both dead, I knew. But she had three brothers—all quite well-to-do. Mitul and Putul always got three sets of new clothes during Eid, in addition to the obligatory dresses that parents were supposed to give. They had been the envy of our childhood, for none of us had ever been able to match their prosperity when Eid came around each year.

'My brothers.' Sharif Aunty enunciated the words without vagueness or emphasis, as if she were parroting a lesson. As if the words were not an answer to a question, or a statement of fact or relationship, but were the conclusion of some certainty, an unerring closing of a door. 'No, I don't think they would take me in.'

My mother did not respond. We all sat there, as still as we could be, as if the slightest careless movement would destroy something precious, invite some under-the-bed monster into the light. The table divided us, the surface cluttered with the debris of our breakfast, the plates in front of our unbidden guests as laden with food as they were empty of hope. No words were spoken for a while, none needed to be said.

Finally, my mother could take the silence no longer. 'You do understand, don't you?' I hated myself for hearing the abjectness in those words, the pleading in the tone, the supplication. I had never heard Ma speak like this.

Sharif Aunty smiled. She reached out and touched my mother's hand. 'I'll find some place, *Bhabi*. It'll be all right. From now on, everything will be fine.' She got up, walked to me and touched my head. 'I'll contact you from wherever I end up. Mitul won't want to lose touch with her friends.'

She walked out of our house. Mitul and Putul followed her without once looking back, without once looking at me. I followed them to the door, watching the awkward grace of the three of them as they took the small footpath that led away from our house.

I heard some movement, and looked back to see my mother swiftly disappearing up the stairs. I walked to the table and sat down to finish my breakfast. Somewhere upstairs a door slammed shut, and then all was silent except for the squidgy noises I made as I chewed and chewed on the bread meant for Mitul and Putul. It seemed important at that moment that the food be consumed, that it not go to waste.

They were gone. They were never heard from again. Oh, there was talk, of course. There was *always* talk. Some of it we heard in the form of whispers and sniggers at school. Some seeped through to us from the guarded and cryptic conversations that the adults had when we kids were around, when they just couldn't hold themselves back. The music teacher was suggested as a possible suspect. After all, how many males—apart from her husband and father-in-law—did this woman encounter in her daily life? And the man—who also gave lessons in a number of houses on the campus—had stopped coming without any prior notice.

But then three weeks after his disappearance, he reappeared just as suddenly with a tedious explanation about how his mother had suddenly died. Various other suspects were considered and discarded. But no one knew for sure. Certainly, Mitul's father searched high and low—as low as could be searched. A police car was seen parked outside their house one morning. The only other time the police had entered the residential area of the campus was when a maid committed suicide for reasons unknown.

The next year, Mitul's father married again. By then, his father had become bedridden, and they needed someone to

take care of him. After all, the way Sharif Uncle was living—
that was no life for a man. Although Sharif Uncle had invited
quite a number of people to his second wedding, my parents
were not among the guests. I don't know what happened to
the new wife. I saw her only once after the wedding. She
was dark and short, with her hair tightly coiled at the base
of her neck. Soon after the marriage, Sharif Uncle took a job
somewhere else and moved away.

Pamela and I missed Mitul, of course. But not as much as
one might think. We had grown used to her absence even
before she left, so her departure was not some sudden sweet
sadness of riven teenage hearts. We would occasionally
wonder aloud where they were, what they were doing,
what had happened to Mitul. Pamela was sure (as was her
mother) that there must have been some man somewhere,
otherwise how could Sharif Aunty have disappeared so
quickly and so effectively?

Our lazy waterside afternoons were not weighted down
with these surmises though. We had other things to do.
For one thing, it was easier doing our joined skipping now.
There was just the two of us, so there was no one to be left
out when we latched onto each other—hands, arms, sides
linked. Pamela had borrowed two books and a purple barrette
with white embossed flowers from Mitul in the summer,
which she had never had the chance to return. Pamela
often worried about them though—the barrette had been
a favourite of Mitul's, and Pamela was very conscientious
about returning things. But that, too, passed.

I never told Pamela about the last time I had seen Mitul.

Something Fishy

Sabrina Fatma Ahmad

'You're filth! Filth! Filthfilthfilthstupidmoronshitfilth!'

The man was obviously a little mad. He stood near the rear doors of the sky train compartment, spouting abuse in his thickly accented English. Speckles of foam formed at the corners of his mouth, and his bloodshot eyes bulged. The other passengers shrank away, but occasionally peeked at him, at once repulsed and fascinated.

Rezia half-turned, and caught a glance from the dark-haired woman seated across from her. The look was equal parts smug, sympathetic, and conspiratorial. That expression, on a face bearing a Mediterranean cast and colouring that was conspicuous amidst the bouquet of North American features, brought to mind the gossipy aunties at weddings back home, with their probing questions and barely concealed malice. *What? Still not married? Bhabi, aren't you getting concerned yet? It's not like she's getting any younger....*

Rezia gave herself a mental shake and smiled back, telling herself it was a little unfair to project her anxieties on a complete stranger like that. After all, this woman probably had better things to do than poke her Grecian nose into someone else's affairs. That was the best thing about coming to British Columbia. It gave her a chance to escape the toxic bitchery that characterised Dhaka society.

As she got off at the Metrotown stop and made for the stairs, the cold fingers of winter leached away the residual warmth of the train compartment, probing through the felt of her coat to poke goosebumps onto her skin. It was an overcast afternoon, as so many here were. The sidewalks glittered with frost, and her breath misted out of her nostrils. By now she had grown fairly accustomed to the climate here, so she continued briskly and confidently onto the sidewalk towards the Metropolis. No, the Burnaby winter wasn't a problem for her anymore; she had felt colder in Dhaka, and not because of the weather. She bit her lip as she thought about the e-ticket she had booked this morning, for a flight back there in four months' time. The prospect did little to improve her mood.

The last time she was back home, a wet-eared graduate from J-school, she figured that an internship at a local law firm would look good on her résumé for when she decided to go into environmental journalism. Convoluted logic, perhaps, but it had made perfect sense to her. A little whining here, a good word there (*Boro Mama* had once been a barrister), and a lot of running back and forth with copies of her CV, finally landed her a stint at Barrister Mrittika Ghoshal's chamber.

She had been prepared for hard work, and wasn't discouraged by the long hours, the abysmal pay, and the endless reading. Interns were low-priority to begin with, and those that lacked a background in law were relegated to something even lower than bottom feeders. Still, she had shored up her resources and worked the elbow grease with the junior lawyers, figuring she would learn a lot. There were days when she had to stay well past midnight, slogging through case files in her cramped cubicle in the book-lined library, the air conditioner slowly turning her into an icicle. The senior partners would order their own dinners, leaving the underlings to fend for themselves. Rezia would have to beg a lift back with a colleague who lived in the same neighbourhood. She would tiptoe into her room so as not to wake her parents, and then collapse into bed for a few precious winks before the 8 am meeting the following day.

The sly glances from the guards, the whispering of the neighbours, and the criticism disguised as concern emanating from her oh-so-well-meaning relatives—these were the stuff of everyday life to her. *Such late hours in the company of unmarried men. It is not seemly, dear. Why don't you find something more appropriate for a girl? How about a nice teaching job? Those private schools pay a lot these days.* She learned to let the talk slide. These were easy lessons compared to the nebulous legal clauses and injunctions she had to bone up on at work.

Her *real* education came from the courtroom, however. She accompanied the junior barristers to the Dhaka High Court one day, when their chamber was looking into a minor criminal case. The whitewashed corridors were swarming with black-robed lawyers and the clerks in their khakis and greys, here and there a harried plaintiff. They were ushered into one of the courtrooms to wait until their case came up, and happened upon another trial in progress. It was a low-profile murder case, the accused a nobody from some backwater in Munshiganj who had butchered his wife and kids. The public prosecutor presented a summary of the charges and brought forth the evidence. It seemed pretty cut and dried. Rezia clutched the wooden railings, leaning

forward in rapt attention to hear what the defence counsel
would have to say.

The lawyer in question was a swarthy man, whose shoe-
polish black hair was slicked back with coconut oil. He
didn't seem the least bit fazed to be on the losing side. He
approached the sleepy-eyed judge, smiling confidently.

'What does your client have to say for himself, Counsel?'

'He made a mistake, M'lord.'

'A mistake, eh? Yes, I suppose you could say that. This
'mistake' could mean life, Counsel.'

'If you please, Your Honour, he didn't know what he was
doing.'

'Well, I can hardly grant bail for that, can I?'

'He won't do this again, Your Honour. He has repented.'

'You make things difficult, Counsel.'

'Please, M'lord...' This last, no doubt, an affectation
inspired by some Kolkata drama serial.

'Oh, all right...'

And just like that, bail was granted. Rezia sat open-
mouthed as the butcher walked out with a smug look on
his face. Whatever happened to legal argument? To *justice*?
Sohel, another intern, caught the look on her face and
motioned her to stay quiet until their case was done. Later,
when she was getting into the office microbus, he pointed at
her cell phone. She read the text message he had sent her,
in response to the question she didn't dare voice. *The defence
counsel is a Party Man*. It made perfect sense: you bat for the
government, and they'll have your back. Outside, there was
blazing sunlight and a windless sky, but sitting in the car,
considering the implications of the text, Rezia was chilled by
the sinking feeling in her stomach.

The soft squelch of mud underneath her boots snapped her back to the present. Her trusty legs had taken over while her mental screen-saver was on, and brought her safely back home. 'Home'—for now—was a cosy flat she shared with the sisters Maha and Malia. She had met the former at the Public Library, near the end of her first year in Canada, and the two had randomly got talking. Phone numbers, and then calls, were exchanged; and the conversations that ensued culminated in the pair moving in with Malia when she shifted out of her uncle's place in Surrey to start her graduate classes in Vancouver. The sisters were easygoing and shared many of Rezia's interests, so it was an ideal arrangement.

Stepping into the welcome warmth of the apartment, Rezia stashed her coat and pottered into the kitchen to be greeted by a briny, mossy stink, a pair of dismayed faces, and a large sock-eye salmon lying on the counter.

'Neha Aunty just got back from a fishing trip and was feeling generous,' Maha answered the unspoken question.

'What do we *do*? I can't cook fish, and neither can Mahappi.'

The fish had glassy eyes and looked singularly disinterested, as if it didn't care about the commotion it was causing.

'I'll do it,' Rezia surprised herself by saying. 'Yeah, I'll take care of it. You girls can do clean-up for a change. I forgot to get the groceries, so one of us would have to go anyway. Why don't you both go? Make a date of it.'

As the sisters shuffled out of the kitchen, Maha paused at the door. 'Are you absolutely positive you don't need us, darling?' she asked.

'I'm sure! Don't worry, it'll be fun.'

'You sure? I thought you hated slaving over a hot stove. Sounds fishy.' This last was accompanied by a comical wiggle of the eyebrows.

'Don't worry about me. You girls run along and enjoy your little shopping spree.'

'Oh, we will.'

Maha winked and left. Rezia stared at the fish lying in the sink. Its dead eyes stared back at her. She blinked first, naturally, not having the advantage of being dead.

'What do I do with you, Fish?'

A mute, unseeing stare was all the reply she got. She sighed and began digging her way through the cookbooks in the kitchen.

As far as she could remember, Rezia had always found excuses to stay away from the kitchen. She blamed it on the smell of curry, on the knives that were never sharp enough, on her fear of the hot oil spitting from her mother's ancient frying pan. Her mother maintained that it was sheer obstinacy on Rezia's part. Rezia suspected that they were both right. Many a fight had broken out in the Sobhan household, with the daughter pleading first homework and then her internship, while the mother wrung her hands, wondering aloud what mother-in-law would ever suffer such a hopeless case. Baba, on the other hand, never got involved.

Coming to Canada for her Masters had been just what she needed. Micro-waved dinners may not have had the flavour of home cooking, but at least she was spared an unhappy marriage to the stove, as she saw it. Maha and Malia had appointed themselves the Kitchen Bitches, while Rezia handled the other chores. It was an ideal arrangement.

She found the instructions for teriyaki salmon in a cut-out

from an article on fusion cooking. It looked simple enough. She began by making a concoction of white wine vinegar, sugar and water to substitute for the white wine listed among the ingredients. Grabbing some fresh ginger and garlic from the fridge, she began to chop. The fish regarded her with a bored expression.

'Just you wait, Fish. When I'm done with you, Ma will have to eat her words. Again.' The absurdity of talking to a dead fish, however fresh it might be, dawned on her, and Rezia smiled and shook her head as she cut the roots down to matchstick sized chips as long as her fingernails.

It had been a rainy weekend the day after the acquittal incident, and the maid had failed to turn up for the third time in two weeks. Ma had been up since morning, cleaning the house, making breakfast and catering to Baba's every whim. Rezia was listlessly dusting the furniture in the family room. She picked up her phone and re-read Sohel's follow-up text, which suggested, not unkindly, that she should get out while she still could. Ma passed by and saw her toss the phone away. She continued on towards the kitchen, shaking her head.

'If it's not the computer, it's the phone. If I ask her, she'll tell me it was work. She probably thinks I'm stupid, that I don't know something fishy is going on.'

All of this was stated with the intention of being overheard. Baba looked up from the paper he was reading, and winked at Rezia, who rolled her eyes. She wasn't going to humour the old man by letting him act like the 'cool dad' today, not when she knew this could only escalate into another spat between her parents.

'...sit on their asses all day, while I wait on them hand and foot...'

Ma's grumbling had become too loud to ignore, and although the rant was ostensibly directed at Rezia, they *all* knew it was intended for Baba—and he was not going to let it slide. His face had already taken on the mulish cast that meant that he was readying for a fight. Rezia took a deep breath and strode into the kitchen. The raw slices of *ruhi* fish for the lunch curry sat gleaming on a tin plate next to the stove. She grabbed a knife and a couple of onions from the cupboard and began to chop. Ma looked up from the ginger and garlic she was mashing and raised an eyebrow.

'Just what do you think you're–'

'Out.'

Rezia's tone left no further room for argument, so her mother took one final anxious look at her fish and walked out. Rezia got busy. Years of watching her mother and the maids, coupled with taste memory, kicked in, and she found herself browning onions, frying fish, and then cooking the gravy as though she had done it all her life. When she served the fish curry at the lunch table, Baba rolled some into a ball of rice and tasted it. 'Perfect. Just the way your mother makes it.'

Ma had surreptitiously wiped away a tear and smiled. 'We'll make marriage material out of you yet.' It was the last time Rezia entered the kitchen.

'All right, Fish. It's time.'

Grabbing it by the tail, she picked it up. It smelled, well, fishy; and for a second, she almost gagged. At least it had been gutted and cleaned, and the scales removed. She cut it into small steaks, and slapped these onto a baking tray, slathered them liberally with the marinade, and then washed her hands.

'Now you ruminate while you marinate. I'm going to take a nap.'

The internship drew to a close, and a burnt-out, jaded Rezia gracefully declined the offer of an extension there. Things had been particularly fraught at home. The big M-word hung in the air. Reassured by the *ruhi* curry episode, Ma had built elaborate castles in the air that involved her daughter preparing feasts, the delicious aromas drawing in suitors by the droves. When Rezia refused to cooperate, feathers began to fly. Baba stayed out of it. As usual. One day, Rezia decided she had had enough of the whole monkey show. She applied to a bunch of grad schools in North America, was accepted by a few, finally decided on the one in British Columbia, and packed her bags. So much for environmental journalism.

Rezia was pulling the baking tray out of the oven when the door opened and the Rahman sisters came traipsing in.

'Mmm... Wow, that smells amazing!'

'Great colour, girl. I can't wait to try this!'

Smiling graciously, trying not to appear too smug, Rezia carefully transferred the smoking fish into a dish, and began to ladle the gravy around it. Malia spotted the small saucer of chopped ginger on the countertop and began to sprinkle it over the fish. Maha loaded the dirty tray and utensils into the dishwasher.

Outside, the soft mist had turned into typical Vancouver rain. The sky slowly darkened to evening, without the fanfare of Dhaka's colourful sunsets. The e-ticket confirmation sat lurking in her inbox, warning of the chaos soon to come. Then Malia cut a slice of fish and popped it in her mouth, pressing index finger to thumb to indicate excellence. And for that moment, it was all that mattered.

Yellow Cab

SRABONTI NARMEEN ALI

'Penn Station, please,' the blonde who stepped into the cab
called out in a whiny voice as she struggled to shut the door
against the wind. Bits of snow floated in and landed on her
soft, fluffy hair.

'Whooooo, it's cold out there, isn't it...' she starts to say,
but the last word dies in her throat with a little croak as
she notices the name plaque on the glass divider in the cab,
accompanied by my picture. Mohammed Khan.

I don't bother answering. By now I know that there's
no point in small talk. Instead I reach over and turn up
the radio. I can see from the rearview mirror that she is
uncomfortable, her teeth biting into cherry-red lips as she
takes out a magazine from her bag and starts to read it. It
takes about fifteen minutes in rush hour traffic to reach her
destination. The meter reads $4.50. I open my mouth to tell
her, but she beats me to it, hurriedly taking out a ten-dollar
bill and passing it to me, careful not to touch me.

'Keep the change,' she says, as she slams the door shut.

Your loss, honey, I think to myself, watching her walk
away, back hunched over to avoid the cold slap of air on her
face. Even through her thick pea coat I can still make out the

full curve of her ass. Mmmmm. Nice. She reminded me of Rebecca, or was it Rachel... something R. The same blonde hair, the same legs, the same pouty lips, cherry flavored, and the same ass. I remember fucking her on my water bed in my bachelor pad on the Upper East Side, heavy breathing, loud moaning, hands grabbing her ass.

I've always been an ass man, from the time I was a teenager in Dhaka. The boys from my school would somehow manage to get hold of a *Playboy* magazine from time to time, and while all my friends were checking out the tits, I would always be looking out for the asses.

But that was a long time ago. Now I am here, in one of the biggest cities in the world, driving a goddamn taxicab. Of all the right and left turns my life has taken since I was a sixteen-year-old, smoking *bidis* by the window of my room in my parents' small flat in Lalmatia—when I was allowed to dream without reality fucking me from behind—I never thought that I would end up here.

My parents were both professors at Dhaka University. My father was head of the Department of Mathematics and my mother was a professor of English Literature. Neither of them was overly religious—they were too busy trying to outdo their friends in intellectual debates—but my paternal grandfather was, hence the name Mohammed. My nickname was Onu and that's what most of my family and friends called me, until the day I got my letter from Harvard University. That's when Onu was murdered quietly in the corner of my hard-top suitcase en route to Boston, via New York, and 'Mo' took his place.

The blare of car horns brings me back to the present.

'Move it, asshole! Can't you fucking see the green light?

Fucking dick!' a passing cabbie screams at me through the closed windows.

New Yorkers are not known for mincing their words. That much is for sure.

I swerve to the side as I see a man in a grey trench coat flagging me down. He opens the door and folds his huge body into the backseat. For a moment, I freeze.

'To Forty-ninth and First, please,' he says, in that deep booming voice that I recognise from my college days.

Gary. Gary Sutton. He was a senior in Harvard when I was a freshman. I doubt that he even knew my name, but I sure as hell knew his. From the moment I stepped onto the campus, I became almost obsessed with him. He was like that alpha male guy in *Revenge of the Nerds*, except he wasn't a dick and he always got the girl in the end. Well, actually, that's probably not the right comparison, but you get the picture.

Six foot three with a quarterback build, sandy hair, and sharp, green eyes encased in metal-rimmed glasses. He was smart, he was funny, he was good looking, and, to top it all off, he was charming as fuck. He was one of those guys who never really let on what they were thinking. He was nice to everyone, but close to no one.

In short, to me, the nerd carrying the tattered leather briefcase that my father gave me as a goodbye present—it had belonged to my grandfather—he was a god. I followed him from a distance during my entire first year. By studying him, I learned how to talk so that other people would listen, how to dress so that other people would notice, how to walk into a room and have everyone turn around and look. For the entirety of my freshman year, aside from working my ass off in my classes, I worked on transforming myself from a 'little Bangla boy', as my roommates would call me, to someone like Gary. Confident, articulate, well-dressed—I erased every trace of my former self, working all-night shifts at the library and morning shifts at the cafeteria so that I could afford expensive clothes, snazzy shoes, and colognes that made the ladies swoon.

I stop at the corner of Forty-ninth and First and he gets out without a second glance, taking a money clip out of his back pocket and handing me a ten-dollar bill.

'Thanks, keep the change,' he says, as he walks away.

Gary Sutton. I had always hoped that I would see him again. Of course, at the time I didn't expect to be driving him to his next destination. I had always thought he would meet the 'new and improved Mo', the man he had unconsciously and unknowingly moulded from scratch.

By the time I graduated from university, I was among the top ten of my year. I landed a job as an investment banker, with a six-figure income. I was made. I moved to New York City, got an amazing apartment within a week. I bought a water bed, the only scrap of Onu that I would allow in my new life—it had been my fantasy from the time I was fourteen years old, and despite leaving so much of myself behind, I still could not get over my water-bed fixation. I worked day and night, had fancy dinners accompanied by women with expensive tastes, invariably taking them back to my water bed. They always left stuff as they hurried out of my apartment in the mornings, still clad in their skin-tight dresses from the night before, their make-up cleaned off their faces and their hair in messy ponytails. I had a collection of hair clasps, sparkly clips, lipsticks, compacts, bracelets, long dangly earrings, and once even a thong with rhinestones.

I barely spent any time at home alone—I was either with a woman, or I was at work. I loved my job. What made it even more amazing was that with one exception, I was the only brown guy in my year. The other brownie, Farid, was a Pakistani from Islamabad. Aside from the fact that his pants were so tight that I suspected he might not be able to have children further down the line, he was a pretty cool guy. We both worked like dogs, subconsciously making up for the fact that we weren't white. And every day I imagined that I would cross paths again with Gary Sutton, and that he would see me as an equal.

Still, the encounter with Gary Sutton wasn't as bad as the one I had last week, when I stopped at a red light and a man in a suit quickly opened the door and got in. I had been about to turn around and tell him to get the fuck out and find another cab. I hated it when people just jumped into my cab without flagging me down first. It was one of the only things I could do that gave me a little power—a remnant of the good old days—but before I could say anything, I realised that I knew him.

'Can you take me to Seventy-ninth and Amsterdam, please?'

Chuck Bernstein, one of my ex co-workers, looked me dead in the face and didn't recognise me, thank god. But then again, why should he? I was a far cry from the clean-shaven Mo he had worked with and downed beers with during Happy Hour at the bar down the street from the office. I automatically retreated into what I like to call my 'Bangu' shell, something put on display for the special customers that I pick up: my shoulders hunched, my eyes blank, and my accent, which I had perfected into a posh New England twang, back into Bangladeshi mode.

'Eeeyeas, Sarrr,' I mumbled.

In my nervousness, I let out a silent fart—the deadly kind that smells. I saw him rolling his eyes through the rearview mirror as he opened the window for some fresh air. I almost laughed out loud. I don't know why it gave me so much pleasure, but I loved making these people uncomfortable. There were some things that only people who have no shame and nothing to lose can get away with. It was almost like the barbarian that had been dormant inside of me for all these years was suddenly back full throttle.

I guess it's not Chuck's fault at the end of the day. He was a pretty all right guy. I had probably spent the most amount of time at work with him, which basically means that I spent most of my waking hours with him. I actually never felt like a brownie with him. It's not his fault that a bunch of crazy Muslim bastards decided to crash into the Twin Towers and kill thousands of people, not to mention destroy thousands of other people's lives. Like mine, to be specific. I got laid off exactly a month after 9/11. They tried to soften the blow by waiting a month, but I knew the day after it happened that my short stint at the top was over. Farid was fired on the same day. We both cleaned out our desks and walked out together, not looking at each other or anyone else.

I saw him a couple of months ago. He was a waiter at Curry in a Hurry on Twenty-eighth and Lexington, where I sometimes treated myself to lunch. The poor fuck was a goddamn Brown graduate, summa cum laude, and he was waiting on taxi drivers from Bangladesh and random white

people who felt like having a little spicy 'Indian' food. We
didn't recognise each other until he took my order of paratha
and egg curry. His pale skin flushed a deep red and I looked
the other way, both of us pretending not to know each other,
neither of us wanting reminders of the lives we had once
had. They were lost to us, distant memories that were more
like dreams than the reality that had been snatched out of
our open hands.

And all for what? For a bunch of terrorist fuckers. God,
how I hated them. I'd heard all the academic explanations
for why they did this, and how historically the Christians
had done the same to them decades or centuries ago,
whichever way you want to look at it. So what? Look at
what the Christians did to the Jews. You didn't see them
fucking killing everyone! They were smarter. They got their
revenge. They learned to brownnose and swindle their way
into everything, and now they own New York. Any killing
they do, they do in Palestine.

To my surprise, my hands are shaking as I remember
last week's incident with Chuck, reliving it as I think about
my encounter with Gary Sutton. I don't believe in God, or
Allah—not anymore, but I have to say there were too many
signs in the past few weeks for me to ignore. I just couldn't
understand what the signs were leading up to, what the
point of all these chance meetings was. I steer the car over
the curb and brake for a moment. As I'm parked I see a *deshi*
girl furiously waving at me, running towards the cab. Her
red coat and matching scarf are fanning out behind her as
she gets in, and I turn around.

'Where to, miss?'

'Onu?'

Oh shit. This is beginning to feel like I'm living in Dickens' tale of Christmas Past—Shaila Chowdhury, my first girlfriend ever, stares back at me.

'Onu, is that you?'

I am tempted to ignore her and turn around, but something makes me stop. I haven't heard the name Onu in ages. It sounded foreign to me, so when I left Dhaka I made my parents start referring to me as Mo. They always sounded hesitant when they called me from Dhaka, saying the name Mo as if they were speaking to a stranger. I hadn't told them yet that I got laid off, because I knew that they would insist that I go back to Bangladesh. I knew I would have to return eventually. I could do this for only so much longer, but I needed more time.

Going back to Dhaka made it too final. I couldn't handle going back when I had spent so much time clawing my way out of my life there, alienating my parents in the process. After I got laid off, I had to leave my apartment in the city and move to a small place in Queens, selling all my unused furniture. The only thing I took with me was my water bed. I told my parents that I had moved because Queens was less intense than the city, and they had taken my word for it. They didn't even suspect that anything was wrong, because that's how far away I had pushed them.

The distance between us was by my need to obliterate any remnants of my life in Bangladesh. My parents, Shaila, my old friends—I had vanished into thin air for all of them, cutting off all ties so that I could move ahead without the chains from my past holding me back. But I guess fate has a way of fucking with me. Fate brought me back to where I started. And now, here she is, the first girl I ever kissed, sitting in the backseat of my cab, looking me straight in the eye and calling me Onu, like all the years in between never happened.

'Shaila,' I croak, my mouth dry. What was it with today anyway?

'How have you been, Onu?' Shaila asks. 'You fell off the face of the earth after the A-levels. No one ever heard from you again.' She acts like this is the most normal thing for me to be doing, like she's not even surprised. I guess living in New York post 9/11 does that to you. You know that anything can happen.

'Good. How have you been? Where to, by the way?' I ask.

'Central Park West. I'm meeting some friends there. Do you want to join us? You'll know some of them.'

'Umm, no, that's okay. I'd rather not.'

'So, Onu, what happened to you? No one ever heard from you after you got into Harvard.'

For some reason I find myself telling her the entire story. From Onu to Mo to Harvard to Gary to work to Chuck. I can't stop talking, and I feel her hands on my shoulders from time to time. She smells amazing, like jasmine.

We get to Central Park and she gives me a tenner, waiting in the backseat as I count out the change. When I hand it to her, she grabs my hands.

'Onu, it's not too late to come back from the dead. We're built to start over, again and again. That's what we do best.'

And with that she walks away, her red coat dotted with snowflakes. I stay there for a long time, watching her go, thinking about what she said. She was always like that, randomly coming out with something really profound, something that would make everyone go quiet and thoughtful.

The ten-dollar bill she gave me is crumpled in my hand. I flatten it out to put it into my wallet and see that she has written her name and number in a bubble coming out of Alexander Hamilton's mouth.

I start the car, and keep an eye out for my next passenger as I drive down the street. The cab smells faintly of jasmine. I open the window to let the smell out.

Pepsi

SHARBARI AHMED

After school, Zara ran into her parents' room to tell her mother about her day, but stopped abruptly when she saw the hard-shell suitcases, semi-packed, on the bed. With a sigh, she dropped her battered backpack with its ballpoint doodles and half-torn stickers to the floor, and sat on the edge of the bed. Her mother was in the bathroom. She heard the toilet flush and the sound of running water. When her mother opened the bathroom door, she saw her daughter, and immediately arranged her face into a pleasing smile. Zara's mother was pretty, more well-kept than anything else, and always, or so it seemed to the little girl, wore a distracted smile. She usually looked over her and around her, but never quite at her.

'Where and how long?' Zara asked in a resigned tone well beyond her ten years.

'Very near,' her mother replied. 'Almost next door. Mombasa.' She kissed the top of Zara's dark head and told her to scoot over, which she did.

An earlier version of this story appeared in *Catamaran Magazine* (USA), December 2003.

'Is it a conference?' she asked. Her mother nodded.

'You didn't say how long for,' Zara added.

'Barely a minute.' Her mother always gave her vague responses that were extreme in their understatement. She talked, the girl thought, like people in black and white British movies set on grand country estates. This had begun to anger her ever since she had turned ten a month before.

'What the hell does that mean?' Zara said violently.

Her mother turned to her, startled, but still smiling. The girl had never spoken like this before. She forgot to reprimand her. 'Well, just five days.'

'Five days!' Zara shouted. 'You are going to leave me alone for five days?'

'Not alone, *Shona*, with Ato Rosa and the cook and…' She stopped when she saw her daughter's face. She could not bear it when the child cried. Out of habit she reached for the bell to ask the housemaid to summon Ato Rosa, their elderly gardener, to calm the girl down, but stopped just in time.

'Don't call me that,' Zara said, sniffing.

'What?' her mother asked uncertainly. '*Shona*? Why? I've called you that since you were a baby. You were just like a little golden dab of humanity.'

'I'm not a baby.'

'That's true,' her mother said cheerily. She walked to the dresser and began rummaging in the lingerie drawers. She pulled out a lacy undergarment still wrapped in pink tissue packaging and held it up to her daughter. 'Do you like it?'

'What is it?' Zara asked in spite of herself. She knew it was a bribe, but was not so self-righteous that she would not be curious about it.

Her mother sat next to her on the bed. 'Panties,' she said.

'Grown-up panties.' She slid them out of their tissue paper and held them up. They were black, with a bit of lace at the waistband.

'I have underwear,' Zara said, unimpressed. 'Mine have Garfield telling the days of the week on them so I can remember what day it is.'

This time her mother's smile was genuine. 'This is not underwear,' she said. 'This is lingerie.'

'What does that mean?'

'Well, it's French, you know. For underwear.' Her mother stopped suddenly and looked properly at her child, whose intelligent eyes were boring into her. Her daughter's eyes always seemed to be demanding something from her. Something inarticulate. Suddenly Zara smiled, relieving the tension, and they both laughed. 'A young lady needs nice things,' her mother said, wagging her finger.

'I guess,' Zara said and shrugged. She took the lingerie from her mother and stood to leave. She knew from experience that whenever her mother resorted to appeasing her with gifts it meant there was nothing more to be said. Her parents were going away again, maybe even for more than five days; her mother was never sure about their itinerary.

Her father was a diplomat. He worked for the UN and, as a result, she and her parents had been travelling since she was a month old. She had lived in three countries in ten years. That meant three different schools and being the new kid three times. That meant no real friends. Before, they had taken her wherever they went. But now that she was older she was left behind, because her mother thought it would be too 'disruptive' otherwise.

Mombasa, in Kenya, was on the water. Zara loved the beach,

especially African beaches of white sand, with water that was as clear as blue-tinted glass. She had been to Mombasa once, and remembered that she had seen schools of tiny, neon-blue fish swimming around her legs and ankles. They had hung together as one body, like one big fish, bobbing in time with the water. When she submerged herself, she wanted to stay under the water; it was so much like what she imagined heaven to be, hushed and clean. Her mother knew how much Zara loved the beach. She was good at her studies; she could have easily missed five days and made it up, no problem.

There was no ocean in Ethiopia, where they lived. To swim, she had to go to the Hilton Hotel's swimming pool every Saturday, which she knew for a fact was not as clean as the waters off Mombasa. All the little children who swam with their mothers holding on to their fat little undersides had pissed in it at least once or twice.

She hated going to the Hilton pool for other reasons. Some of the kids from her class would be there, ignoring her and enjoying themselves. Sometimes one of the kids would have a birthday party. That was the worst, because chances were she would not be invited. They all swam together in the pool and cheered her on when she did cartwheels off the low diving board. But afterwards, when it was time for cake and games, they would run off and she would be left alone.

As for water, Ethiopia was a thirsty place. There were natural hot springs in Awash that were cool enough in some parts so that people could swim, and Zara had to admit that was the most beautiful, magical underwater world she had ever seen. Their guide had told them that it was the cleanest water in Africa. When she looked down she could see her feet clearly, nut brown against the white, shimmering sand.

She loved Ethiopia and most parts of her life. The country held her imagination hostage. It was mostly a land of craggy mountains and honey-coloured savannahs, but she thought the starkness of the bare mountains the most beautiful. Zara knew it to be a holy place, maybe even where the Ark of the Covenant was hidden deep in the bowels of an ancient church. That was what she had been told by Ato Rosa, their gardener. Indiana Jones had gone rummaging in the wrong place, Zara thought in wonder a year later in a darkened theatre, as she watched the rumpled hero battle the Nazis for the coveted relic. In real life, a silent man clad all in white guarded this church day and night. Before he died, he would name his heir. No modern eyes had seen what it was that he and his heirs guarded, but it seemed everyone old enough to remember knew it existed and was certain it was there.

There had once been a king in Ethiopia—the Lion of Judah, they called him—who wore a cloak and held a sceptre, like something out of a fantasy. Zara believed everything that was said about Haile Selassie, the last great African king— how he tossed coins of gold with the image of a crowned lion embossed on one side out into the crowds thronging to see him, how he bathed in milk and in the blood of his enemies, and how he drank urine. The house Zara now lived in had once belonged to his daughter, a real princess, but she herself had never lived there.

Zara got most of her information about life from her father, Ato Rosa, and the Nancy Drew Mystery books—in that order. On their yearly camping trips to Lake Langano, she and her father would light a fire in the sand and he would settle down to tell her stories. The year she turned nine, he sat her in his lap and told her that he had come to Ethiopia because so many people were dying of famine. He told her what a tragedy this really was because, between the corrupt leadership of a man named Mengistu Haile Mariam and the drought that had killed nearly all the cattle and destroyed the crops, the people were slowly being defeated.

But the Ethiopians were not easy to defeat. They were among the only Africans never to have been colonised. This made them proud and self-confident in a way that many people from many countries could never be. Because of this pride, her father told her, they had faced Mussolini's tanks with spears and shields wrapped in lion skin and were not vanquished.

'No one ever told the Ethiopians that they were not as good as anybody else, Zara. Which is why they could win a battle like that.'

To Zara, it all made perfect sense because it sounded like a story from the Bible, and this was where (according to Ato Rosa) the Bible was invented.

'The Ethiopians are very brave, right, Daddy?' Zara had asked her father. He nodded, his face, a face Zara loved utterly, thoughtful in the glow in the fire. 'But now, Zara baby, as brave as they are they are killing each other in a civil war, up north in Eritrea, and dying from famine. They are dying from the inside.' Zara would remember how sad her father had looked that night.

Zara always enjoyed herself at the lake and the hot springs in Awash. But still, she did not relish being left behind while her parents went away to be near an ocean. She longed to sit on a beach with her father and drip wet sand through her fingers and build whimsical, lopsided towers of sand that looked as if they were made from vanilla ice cream.

She wanted to snorkel all day and bake in the sun until her mother called out in alarm, 'Come in at once! You'll be as dark as midnight!'

Her mother was proud of her fair skin and often lamented (smiling the whole time) the slightly duskier complexion Zara had inherited from her father. It was June, and the school year would end in just two weeks. They could have waited for me, Zara thought. But I guess the conference couldn't wait. She vowed to spend the entire five days outside so that when her mother returned, she would be in for a rude shock at how dark her daughter had become. Her goal was to be darker than the housemaids, which was not very hard as most Ethiopians were light-skinned.

'You can spend Saturday night at Jennifer Duschene's house if you want. I've already spoken to her mother.'

'No thanks,' Zara scowled. Jennifer was the Canadian ambassador's daughter, and very proud of her status as an ambassador's daughter. Zara and she spent much time play-acting, and she was always a mere subject or a criminal begging for a reprieve while Jennifer was either the Queen or Prime Minister.

'I've met Trudeau,' Jennifer once boasted, and Zara, who was an avid reader of comic strips, was impressed at first.

'Really? I love 'Doonesbury'! Sometimes I don't understand all the jokes, though. My dad says I will if I read up on current events.'

'No, you ninny!' the imperious Jennifer replied after a baffled silence. 'Prime Minister Trudeau. You're so weird.'

Zara preferred to read during recess, or at least pretend to read. It spared her the humiliation of being ignored when teams were picked for kick ball.

Everyone disliked Jennifer because she was so snooty and that was why she sought out Zara, another outcast. It was not that Zara was very disliked, at least not as much as Jennifer was. It was simply that none of her classmates knew what to make of her. She was too brooding and earnest. It made them uncomfortable.

Zara knew that if Jennifer, her only friend, ever managed to gain favour, she would be dropped. And not only dropped, but treated more cruelly by her than any of the other children, because she was a reminder of Jennifer's less glorious past. That was what Ato Rosa told her to expect. It was the nature of politics, he explained.

'The sooner you know about human politics,' he told her, 'the better. When people are not sure of who they are, they hate the ones who see through them.'

Zara did not completely understand what the elderly man meant, but she knew that Jennifer was a bit mercenary. Zara's mother couldn't have been happier about their friendship because Jennifer's mother was a great favourite of hers. For the most part, Zara was grateful for Jennifer's companionship. It was only when she made personal comments about her and her mother that she found herself feeling hostile.

'Why does your mother always wear that scarf to parties?' Jennifer asked Zara one day.

'It's not a scarf, dodo, it's a sari,' Zara said, exasperated.

'Aren't you American?' Jennifer challenged. 'Americans don't wear saris.'

'My parents are from Bangladesh, but I am an American,' Zara said uncertainly. It sounded more like a question than a statement. 'They are citizens. They have passports.'

Jennifer, like the seasoned politician she would eventually

become, saw the weakness and went in for the kill. 'Well, all the Americans *we* know don't speak with accents and wear weird clothes. All the Americans *we* know go to church.'

'No thanks,' Zara said again when her mother tried to coax her into going to Jennifer's house for a sleepover. 'I'll stay here. Alone,' she added dramatically.

'All right, but I do wish you would be nicer to Jennifer. She is such a sweet girl,' her mother sighed. She looked at her daughter, bedraggled as she often was after school, and wished she could say more to her. She could never find the right words for her daughter. In her darker moments she had to admit that Zara was a stranger to her, and so different from how she herself had been at that age. Zara always asked questions that stymied her. Her husband was generally able to answer their daughter's questions with ease, but lately he, too, had been preoccupied with work, and Zara seemed more distant and resentful than usual.

Zara walked downstairs and into the garden to look for Ato Rosa. He was burning leaves in a far corner of the compound. Ato Rosa's left eye was always tearing from a childhood injury. He constantly dabbed at it with a blue handkerchief he kept in his pocket. He had a tiny moustache just above his upper lip; it was so small, the girl had first mistaken it for an insect. It was really more of a tiny tuft of hair than a moustache. He wore a threadbare beige sweater bordered in dark brown, with a white t-shirt underneath, and forest-green corduroy pants that were worn at the knees and duly patched up. This was his work uniform. Zara could not recall ever seeing him in anything else since he had come to work for them, over two years earlier.

He took off the battered cap Zara's father had given him

during his first week with them and wiped his forehead with it. There were bits of dry leaves stuck in his curly silver hair. He wiped his eye with the back of his thumb.

Suddenly Zara felt guilty. 'I could have helped you rake the leaves,' she said.

'I finished before you got home. What's going on?' Ato Rosa asked her in Amharic. He could see that she was forlorn yet again.

'Nothing,' she replied, also in Amharic, and shrugged.

'It's only for five days,' he said gently, and waved the smoke away with a piece of cardboard as it began to waft towards her.

'That's what Mommy says, but she always gets it wrong. They'll probably be gone a month.'

Ato Rosa patted her head and bent down, with difficulty, to sift the smouldering ashes under the leaves.

'My mother once left me when I was a little boy,' he said, beginning a familiar tale that Zara almost had memorised. 'It was for a good reason. She came to me in the early hours of the morning and said, 'Son, I am going to Jerusalem. I will be back in six weeks.'

'Mombasa is like a resort,' Zara said, sighing. 'They have swimming pools with waterfalls.'

'We Jews can't stay in one place for very long,' Ato Rosa said as if he hadn't heard her. 'We really are nomadic.'

'Mommy and Daddy aren't Jewish, they're Muslim.'

Ato Rosa looked at her. 'Same difference,' he said, smiling. 'We all came from the desert.'

'At school when I told Ms Pfister what you said about Ethiopia being Judah and where the original Jews came from, she said that all Jews came from Israel.'

'No, no, Ms Pfister is wrong. That's where all Jews want to end up, but that's not where they all came from,' Ato Rosa said. He looked at her speculatively. 'This Ms Pfister, she's German?'

Zara shook her head. 'Nope. She's from Sandusky, Ohio. Is that why your mommy went to Palestine? To die?' she asked suddenly.

It was both Zara's and Ato Rosa's habit to interchange Palestine and Israel. They could keep track. Ato Rosa had told her it was just different names for the same place.

'Yes,' Ato Rosa replied.

Ato Rosa's mother never came back after six weeks. She died in Jerusalem. She had been very sick he had told the little girl, but not to frighten her. He pointed out that her parents always came back and never went away for six weeks, and they appeared to be in no immediate danger of dropping dead.

'Do you want to go to Jerusalem?' Zara asked fearfully. She could not help being afraid; she would always equate going to Jerusalem with death and being left behind, because of Ato Rosa's story—even when she grew up.

Ato Rosa looked at her earnestly and shook his head. 'Why should I? This is my home,' he said slowly. 'I'm not going anywhere.'

'You said all Jews want to end up there.'

'We all do someday,' he replied, winking mysteriously. He stood up with difficulty, his arthritic knees nearly buckling from the effort. 'Go play now, girl. I have to muck out Tinnish's stall.'

'I'll help you,' Zara said. Tinnish was her pony, which she had outgrown, and was very neglected by her. This was the only thing that Ato Rosa held against her, and Zara knew this.

'Not today,' he said. 'Go play.'

'With who?' Zara said in a soft voice and looked around.

Ato Rosa looked back at her and dabbed at his bad eye with a soiled handkerchief.

'Listen,' he said, pointing to the sky. She did—and eventually she heard the sound of children's laughter and high-pitched squeals coming from just over the ivy-covered wall that enclosed the compound.

'But they're outside,' she said.

'So are you,' he said and walked into the stable.

'I meant they're outside the wall,' she called after him.

'To them, so are you,' Ato Rosa replied, poking his head out of the stable.

Zara scrambled up the high wall by lodging her toes in the cracks between the stones and managed (as she had many times before) to reach the top. She had watched the children play before, but had never been inclined to join them because she thought they wouldn't let her. Why should they be any different from the kids at school? They had arrived one morning a few weeks earlier—and suddenly overnight, in the dusty clearing, there was a makeshift shanty town constructed of bits of corrugated tin and a great deal of cardboard.

In the two years Zara had been living in the house, there had been two such temporary towns next door, but nothing as big as this one.

Jennifer's mother, who lived on the next road, lamented to Zara's mother one day, 'This one seems permanent.' She claimed that they stole water from all of them by digging down to their wells and diverting a little bit of it every day, but Zara's parents didn't seem to mind, or even to really believe her. There was a small river, shrouded by a thicket of skinny eucalyptus trees that ran just beyond their camp. That was probably where they did their washing and bathing and probably also where they got their drinking water, which was not very drinkable. Zara had got blood dysentery from drinking out of that very river. She had to eat boiled rice and carrots for two weeks straight.

The children, who were all ages, from four to fourteen, were playing a game called Pepsi. A circle was drawn in the sand and seven Pepsi bottle caps were stacked up in the centre of it. Two teams were formed, usually after much negotiation, with one team's objective being to knock the stack down and then re-stack it without being hit with a ball by the other team. Being hit meant being disqualified. If all team members attempting to re-stack were tagged, then the game was over, but if a team member could successfully re-stack the caps without being tagged, then they yelled Pepsi! And victory was declared.

Pepsi was not a game for the faint of heart or the mal-coordinated, as far as Zara could see. One had to be dexterous, and able to contort oneself so as not to get tagged. The tags were not mere love taps. They were delivered so as to be murderously accurate and to inflict as much damage as possible. The head and groin areas were not off-limits.

At first Zara could not understand what was making the children yelp whenever they got hit, because the ball was made out of rolled-up socks. Then she saw one of the players—a tall girl, probably the oldest one—stop to re-wind and fortify the ball with small pebbles and a sharp-edged

Pepsi cap placed just underneath the first layer of cloth. It was merciless and bloody, unlike anything she had ever seen on the International Community School playgrounds.

She ached to play. No one seemed to see her perched on top of the wall, hugging her worn denim-covered knees and rocking back and forth. She could just call out and ask to be included, draw attention to herself somehow. Would they think her strange or laugh at her, she wondered. She looked down at her grimy jeans and orange t-shirt with its holes and was suddenly self-conscious. In her child's way, she failed to notice that most of the children playing were barefoot and wore torn clothing, and that all of them were filthy.

She decided to climb back down. It was too hard to ask to be included. If someone had approached her, she would have readily participated. She looked over the edge and wondered if she could jump back into the garden. It wasn't that high; a metre, she surmised. And then someone tapped her on the shoulder.

'Want to play?' It was a boy, all eyes and bones, barely seven years old, with close-cropped hair and a thin white scar that ran across his dusty brown forehead. He was shirtless, but wore a pair of battered sneakers with no laces in them. He looked like the boys who stood at the intersections on the main roads in the city and gestured towards their open mouths with dirty fingers and moaned. When they had first come to Addis Ababa, her mother always carried a separate change purse in which she put coins to hand out to people whenever they went out. But she had stopped doing that a while back, on the advice of Jennifer's mother and her bridge club.

The boy had scrambled expertly up his side of the wall,

and now stood behind her. In her surprise, Zara nearly fell back, but the boy caught her by the arm.

He studied her thoughtfully with old eyes and then said, 'Do you have a sock?'Zara nodded mutely. 'Go get it,' the boy said. 'Please,' he added as an afterthought. He looked out over the garden. Zara saw his eyes taking in the sprawling lawn and the glass-and-stone house built into the hillside; the horses grazing lazily in a lower part of the garden; the bright yellow and magenta 'desert rose' Schwinn bicycle left carelessly by the side of the driveway; the dogs tumbling around and yipping at each other. Between the flowers and the toys and the animals, the garden was a riot of colour, a wonderland. Even Zara saw it when her more accustomed eyes followed his around the property. Off to one side was a long-forgotten rope swing with a piece of wood tied to it for a seat. It hung from the branches of a baobab tree and swayed gently in the breeze. The boy's round eyes lit up when he saw the swing. But it was brief. His face soon took on its previous detachment.

'We need a sock. The ball is ripping,' he said and picked his nose with a black pinkie nail. He waggled the finger around a bit before flicking dried snot into the grass and looked at her. Spittle gathered at the corners of a cracked mouth that hung perpetually open. Zara could hear him breathing through his stuffed nose. She climbed down the wall.

'Can I play?' she called up to him.

The boy shrugged a skeletal shoulder. 'Are you good at Pepsi? It's a hard game.'

'I've never played before,' she said, looking embarrassed.

He reached into the front of his torn shorts and scratched

himself, pondering the weight of the information he had just been given.

'Who's that?' he asked, pointing towards the stable.

Zara looked over her shoulder. She waved to Ato Rosa, who was watching them.

'That's Ato Rosa,' she said. 'He takes care of the horses and the garden ... and me,' she added.

'What kind of a name is Rosa? It's a girl's name,' the boy snorted. 'It's not Amharic.'

'I know,' Zara said. 'He worked for an English woman before and she couldn't pronounce his name, so she changed it.'

'You speak Amharic. It's not very good, though,' he added pointedly, so that she didn't get the idea he was impressed with her in any way. 'Why don't you call him by his real name?'

'I don't know his real name,' Zara said, looking down at her feet. She glanced towards the old gardener, who was no longer watching them, but was busy untangling the pony's mane with a curry-comb.

'Well, go get the sock,' the boy ordered.

'Can I play?' she asked again.

'Yes, I guess so.' He turned and climbed back down his side of the wall.

Zara ran, elated, up the driveway and into the house. She raced up the stairs two at a time to her room and yanked open a drawer where pairs of socks were rolled into neat balls and placed side by side, according to colour, down the length of it. She scratched her elbow and stared at them. The maid who took care of all of her things would be very upset if she took one of her socks and gave it to the boy.

Zara could tell she didn't like her very much. She would snitch on her.

Zara walked into her mother's room. The suitcases were now packed and shut. Her mother's beauty box with all her toiletries was open on the dresser, and her mother had started packing it.

'Yes?' her mother said, smiling at her standing in the doorway.

'Could I have one of your pantyhose?'

'Why?'

'Uh, I'm going to play dress-up.' The lie came easily and she felt only the tiniest twinge of guilt. The sight of the suitcases on the bed dispelled it a second later, however.

'Well,' her mother hesitated. She walked to the dresser and then turned around. '*Shona*? What happened to the other pair I gave you when Jennifer came over?'

'I don't know,' the girl snorted. 'That was ages ago.'

The mother decided, rather uncharacteristically, that she was not going to indulge her daughter.

'Sorry, dear, but I can't just keep giving you things only to have you lose or damage them.'

Zara's eyes narrowed and she scowled at her mother, who was immediately contrite. They were leaving her, after all, for several days. Maybe even two weeks—she just couldn't be sure about the itinerary. But before she could say anything, Zara stormed out, shouting, 'Never mind. I don't need it!'

Zara sat on her bed and sighed. If she showed up without a sock, they wouldn't let her play. And suddenly it was very important to her to be allowed to play Pepsi. She knew she would be good at it and she could teach her classmates to play it during recess. She imagined herself playing Pepsi with Marit Brandsma and Kevin Mfume–Stone, who was always boasting about being related to David Livingstone because his mother was Rhodesian and his father was English, and all the other cool kids, who would think her great for making up this brilliant, brutally exciting game.

No need to tell them where I learned it, she thought shrewdly. I could take credit for it. But she really needed to play it in order to speak with any authority about it, because she knew Kevin would challenge her, as he did everyone.

She had decided to take a pair of socks out of the drawer and deal with the consequences, when her eyes fell on the pink tissue package that was lying next to the bed. Her mother walked into the room just then and asked her if she still wanted the pantyhose, but Zara shook her head and gave her a winning smile. 'It's okay, Mommy,' she said. 'I shouldn't have bothered you.'

She slid the panties out and gave the elastic waistband a snap when her mother had left her room, and thought, 'This will do.'

When Zara handed the panties to the tall girl she had seen re-wrapping the ball earlier, everyone looked down at the underwear sceptically. A moment before they had all been staring at her, some of them slack-jawed, when Zara had greeted them. '*Tenest-elin*, how are you?' she said. They had been between games and in the process of choosing new teams when Zara climbed down their side of the wall. No one greeted her back or asked for her name. She didn't mind that, or the staring. She just wanted to play.

'What is it?' Esther, the rather taciturn leader of the group asked, turning the lacy panties over.

'Underwear,' Zara replied. 'You put your legs through the holes and wear it.'

'It's not thick enough,' Esther said. 'It'll tear.'

'The elastic is good,' Zara said, demonstrating by snapping it once, hard. 'You can use it to fling the ball.' The kids, seven in all, murmured to each other as she waited. Zara could not completely understand them. Their accents were very different from Ato Rosa's or the rest of the house staff.

She looked over their heads at the 'town' behind them. Up close, it looked even more temporary and thrown together. A small child cried relentlessly into the silence from somewhere in the maze of cardboard, bits of corrugated tin, wood, and rags. The smell of kerosene hung in the air. She saw a grown-up emerge from one of the shelters, a woman with a red scarf wrapped around her head, carrying a naked baby low on her hip. The baby whined, and the woman pulled her shirt up and roughly shoved a swollen purple nipple into the baby's mouth.

'Aw, let her play,' the boy she had first spoken to said. 'Now the teams will be even. I can count,' he added proudly for Zara's benefit.

Esther, the leader, nodded her assent, and said, 'Okay, but no going easy on her just because she's new. And she talks funny. I don't like that.'

'She's from the outside,' the boy said. They all looked at Zara, who gazed shyly at her feet.

'Where's she from?' Esther asked the boy.

'I don't know,' the boy said. 'She's dark, maybe she's from Djibouti or maybe she's an Arab,' he said in a burst of inspiration.

'I'm American,' Zara said, with hesitation.

'In America, everybody's white,' Esther said, her pretty honey-coloured face suddenly distrustful.

'That's not true,' Zara said vehemently.

'Who cares if she's Haile Selassie?' the boy said. 'Let's play.'

Zara was not spared Esther's surgical attacks on the buttocks and calves. She could feel the pebbles and sharp-edged bottle cap cutting into her. But she was swiftly able, as she had known she would be, to dodge the ball easily. Soon she was adept at stacking the bottle caps with precision and speed, and both teams vied for her when it came time to pick sides. Her heart sank as the sun set and it became harder to see the ball, or even the bottle caps. Esther threw her slim arm around Zara's shoulders, and invited her to eat *injira* with her family. The girl loved the spongy grey bread, especially with *birbire*, even though the ground chili powder made her eyes water and mouth sting, but she said she had to go home. She felt tears of regret prick her eyes as she said this.

'Come tomorrow,' Esther said, slowly, so that Zara would understand her. She observed her thoughtfully. 'You can be captain. But bring a sock this time. None of that fancy underwear stuff.'

'Really? I can be captain?' Zara could hardly believe it. Never in her ten years had she been captain.

'Yes, why not?' Esther sniffed dismissively. 'It's hard work, though. You have to control your team. These fools are not easy to control.'

They looked at the rest of the children, some of whom were pushing and shoving one another for no apparent reason. One boy cuffed his small sister on the head and giggled in glee when she began to cry. The offering of lingerie Zara had brought had been discarded long before as being too slippery and lay tattered, next to them. One of the children picked it up and quickly stuffed it into his pocket to show his mother.

Zara climbed wearily up the wall before glancing back one last time at the shantytown. Lanterns were being lit as mothers gathered up their children for what she knew would be a meagre meal. Probably all they would be eating that night was *injira*, with no meat or vegetables. The candles flickered in the dying daylight. She had lost sight of Esther. She was scratched and sore, but happy in a way she had never been. She glanced in satisfaction down at her torn knee—an injury sustained early on in the game.

As she walked slowly up the driveway to her house, the lamps lining the driveway turned on as if by magic. Zara imagined they had lit up for her, a champion returning home after a long day in the arena. There was tomorrow, she thought with happy anticipation. And with it, a new game of Pepsi, with no parents and no one to tell her she had to come home early. Maybe tomorrow, she would share *injira* with Esther's family, and maybe tomorrow she could steal a whole chicken from the larder, and some carrots and some butter, and definitely some bottles of Pepsi for reinforcements.

The front door opened just as she was reaching for the doorknob. Her mother stood glaring down at her, her face streaked with tears and mascara. Beside her stood Jennifer's mother, who looked at her with a mixture of contempt and pity. Zara saw Ato Rosa holding his hat and standing in the hall behind his mistress. The house staff's look of alarm changed to resentment when they saw the girl was filthy, her t-shirt torn. She could tell that her mother had been berating them for some time. Zara looked quickly at Ato Rosa, who winked at her with his good eye. Her heart began beating fast.

'My God, *hai Allah*!' the girl's mother said, her voice squeaky with hysteria, as she pulled Zara in by her arm. 'Where have you been? How could you do this to me? We have missed our flight. We have called the police. These incompetent people!' her mother said, pointing at the house staff and at Ato Rosa. 'No one saw where you went. I know why you did this, but this is not right. Your father is very upset.' And on and on she went. Zara did not know how long she had been playing Pepsi on the other side of the wall, so she asked her mother, who looked at her as if she were mad.

'Four hours!' she cried. She could not control the disgust in her eyes as she looked at her daughter's grimy face and dirty fingernails. It was a look she reserved for street dogs and errant servants. Zara saw it and, for the first time in her life, she wanted to hit her mother. Just slap her the way she had seen women in movies do. Her mother shoved her towards the housemaid, who was then instructed to bathe her. 'We can still catch the next flight, but you have to be quick, missy!' She turned to Jennifer's mother and asked her to hold her assignments for her.

'But I can't go!' Zara cried, dismayed.

'Oh? And why suddenly not?'

'Because I have plans!' she said. She heard Ato Rosa's low, dry cough and looked behind her mother at the old man. He shook his head at her and frowned. The girl caught his eyes, but ignored him, even when he coughed again.

'Do something about that cough, Ato Rosa!' Zara's mother snapped, running her fingers nervously through her hair. She regretted, at that moment, hiding the fact that she smoked. She was tempted to light up right there, in front of her daughter and the maid, who stole cigarettes from her regularly.

'Yes, ma'am,' he replied to her back, replacing his hat, which he always removed out of respect when he entered the main house.

'Don't tell me about plans, missy!' her mother said. 'Mine have been ruined by your selfishness.'

Zara's face took on a look of stubborn resolve. 'I have to play Pepsi tomorrow with Esther. I promised. I'm bringing the socks.' She heard Ato Rosa's sigh.

'I don't understand you. Who's Esther?' her mother said, not entirely hearing what Zara had said because at that moment the police were ringing the doorbell. She nodded towards the maid. 'Miriam will help you pack. You can have as much Pepsi as you want on the plane.'

Miriam—young, pretty, and resentful of her station in life—dragged the protesting girl up the stairs. At the top of the stairs, when she was sure no one was looking, she gave Zara's hair a yank. Downstairs, Ato Rosa made a mild attempt to intervene on Zara's behalf. He was sharply rebuked. He watched helplessly as Zara stood at the top of the stairs and cried, before she was pulled away by the maid.

The shiny black car wound slowly down the lit driveway and through the gate. Zara was going to Mombasa, just as she had wanted to that very afternoon. Her father had been informed of the day's events. He wouldn't have minded really, he had whispered to her mother in the car, if they had taken another flight. They were arriving early either way.

As they passed the clearing where Esther and the others lived, Zara strained to catch a glimpse of a familiar face, but all she saw were flickering lights dancing in between the flimsy cardboard walls and tin shanties. Everyone was inside eating their *injira*, probably sitting around a colourful woven basket and eating the bread communally with their fingers. By the time Zara returned from Mombasa, she would be forgotten. She would have to prove herself all over again.

She turned to look through the back window one last time. A white and black police van drove right into the clearing. Five men, waving batons, jumped out of the back and ran towards the shanties. She heard the faint sound of police whistles. She found she could not cry out. She looked at her parents, who were quietly arguing, oblivious to the drama unfolding behind them. Zara turned around and slid down the leather seat until her feet touched the floor of the car. She began to cry silently. She looked up to see her mother staring at her, but the girl's steady gaze, brimming with recrimination, made her mother look away.

Zara closed her eyes. Her mind became a tumult of thoughts and images. Ato Rosa had told her what the police could do. She saw Esther cowering in fear, with the smaller children behind her. Her friends. She knew somehow that they would not be there when she returned, and the thought was almost too much to bear. She scrambled into her father's lap. Just as the car turned on to the main road, a shot rang out in the still, dry air, and Zara winced.

Getting There

FARAH GHUZNAVI

Laila realised she had to get a grip when she caught herself sighing for the third time in five minutes. She desperately needed to talk to someone, and the few friends who qualified were out of reach. Their much-anticipated girls' night out the previous week had receded to a faraway fragment of memory, eclipsed by the jolt of more recent events. Those celebrations now felt as if they belonged in an unattainably distant past.

The car ride was the first opportunity she had had to hear herself think since things fell apart, and her body seemed to be using the breathing space literally, drawing in as many deep breaths as possible. Despite the vehicle's quietly efficient air-conditioning system, Laila's skin felt heated. A sense of irritation prickled along her tightly stretched nerves—as if irreverent fingers were teasing a set of piano keys, every now and then hitting a grinding note of disharmony, as the seriousness of the situation struck her anew.

An earlier version of this story appeared in the *Lady Fest* e-book (Dead Ink Publishers, UK) and in *Curbside Splendor Issue 2* (Curbside Splendour, Chicago, USA) 2011. The story was awarded second place in the Oxford Gender Equality Festival Short Story Competition in 2010.

Despite her unease, it was an enormous relief to be heading back to Dhaka. The Bangladeshi capital felt like home to Laila in a way that the port city of Chittagong never had. Leaving the task of negotiating the treacherous highway traffic in her driver's able hands, she cast another furtive look back at the children. They lay with their tawny golden limbs sprawled untidily in all directions, taking up the spacious rear of her new Honda Accord.

She couldn't help wondering what she had let herself in for, although the accident had left her little choice. But there were good reasons why she had decided never to have children, she thought ruefully, and now she had two on her hands! It was bad enough having to deal with a teenager (in Laila's limited experience, this was a period that manifested itself in ways similar to a disease rather than a stage of growth), but she felt even less confident in handling the younger child, who appeared to have temporarily fallen silent.

Six-year-old Aliya had finally, mercifully, gone to sleep. Just in time. Her repeated queries about how much longer the trip would take had been interrupted only by supplementary questions as to why she had to go *anywhere* with her unfamiliar aunt. Laila sympathised with her niece's feelings, but it didn't help an already awkward situation. She was finding the journey interminably long herself, made worse by the frequent slowdowns in traffic whenever they approached a bridge or passed through yet another small town.

Each time, the noise level went up. Crowds of pedestrians swirled past the vehicle as it inched its way forward, its passengers hemmed in by the raucous crush of strangers. Hawkers paused briefly to display their wares—paper-wrapped cones of hot, sand-roasted peanuts in the shell, improbably bright pink and green sweets, cheap plastic toys, unpeeled hard-boiled eggs (always the safest bet, to avoid stomach bugs), and multicoloured hair-bands. Every so often beggars tapped pleadingly against the determinedly rolled-up windows, leaving behind smears on the glass as ghostly reminders of their passing presence.

After her interrogation failed to extract satisfactory answers, Aliya began making increasingly impassioned demands to return home, all of it exacerbating Laila's already unsettled frame of mind. She held on to her impetuous temper with some difficulty. It was only after they had finally reached an open stretch of the highway, and relative quiet prevailed, that exhaustion finally caught up with the youngster.

In a contrast that could not have been starker, Aliya's teenage sister, Yasmin, had neither questions nor demands for their aunt. Laila calculated that Yasmin had not uttered more than two consecutive sentences since their abrupt re-introduction a few days previously. Not strange, of course, given that she was still in shock. An intelligent fourteen-year-old, the implications of what was happening could not have been lost on her.

Now, accidentally making eye contact with the older girl as she threw another compulsive look backwards, Laila observed the guarded expression on the teenager's shuttered face. Clearly Yasmin understood all too well what was happening, and why. Trying to deflect Laila's annoyance during Aliya's earlier tirade, she had said, pleadingly, 'Don't mind Aliya. She's just tired, you know, and a little scared.'

With that, the teenager had lapsed back into what Laila was beginning to think of as her characteristic silence. Just as well. The emotions simmering below the surface of their mundane exchanges rendered hollow any pretence of normality.

Yasmin's reticence was perfectly understandable, Laila conceded. Their lack of familiarity had been brought sharply into focus by this unexpected, unwelcome proximity, something that would have been problematic even without the emotional carnage left lingering in the wake of recent events.

Laila's mind drifted inexorably back to the point where her life had started to spiral awry—just seventy-two hours and a lifetime ago. She was having a night out with her closest girlfriends after way too long. The five of them were increasingly caught up in their hectic individual lives—careers on the upswing, family dramas, a boyfriend or two—so get-togethers had become few and far between. The group played a particularly important part in Laila's life, since, unlike the others, she had no time for romance. She hadn't broken the chokehold of her father's control to risk replacing it with another entitled male in her life, however silken the glove disguising *that* handsome fist might be.

Laila was treating everyone to a lavish evening out at the cutting-edge sushi bar that had opened recently at one of the city's five-star hotels. Their get-together was in honour of a lucrative contract secured by the architecture firm for which she worked. They were to build another of the ubiquitous shopping malls mushrooming amidst the unmanageable urban snarl-up that was Dhaka. Their challenge would be to design something unique and eye-catching, in line with their rapidly developing reputation.

The evening was hugely enjoyable. The exquisitely crafted

Japanese morsels were colourful and delicious, exceeding expectations, and the accompanying sake flowed its smooth, riverine way into cups raised repeatedly in celebration, no one keeping track of how much made its way into their internal channels. It was, after all, a girls' night out—and a damn good one at that!

Returning home several glorious hours later, Laila cast a cursory glance at her mobile phone. To her dismay, there were twenty-three missed calls buzzing in her call-list like an angry swarm of bees. If the number of incoming calls had not been sufficient to signal an approaching storm, the area code displayed for the city of Chittagong left her in no doubt that she would not like what was heading her way.

The sound level at the event had been raucous, high spirits and other spirits combining to melt the edges of her normally alert senses into a warm caramel haze. Otherwise the racket from the mobile would have been unmissable. Mentally berating herself for the time lost—the digits from the persistent number flashing in red neon lights through the haze enveloping her tired brain—she called back immediately.

The reassuring solidity of the mahogany dining table provided much-needed support, though Laila was not conscious of leaning against it as she listened to her mother's splintered voice spilling out the story: about her sister Shaheen, an accident on the highway, and the clinical silence of the intensive care unit as a terrified family huddled together for comfort, waiting for news.

'Where *were* you? We've been trying to reach you for hours! You're never there when you're needed! And why did you pick up the phone now, so late at night?' Ma said accusingly. Despite an instinctive sense of resentment at her mother's tone, Laila registered her usual Pavlovian response, stammering an apology as waves of guilt shuddered through her.

This was why she had left Chittagong, she couldn't help thinking, with more than a little bitterness. Not that she would ever have allowed herself to articulate that thought out loud. As she had done for so much of her adolescent life, she kept it tucked safely away in the inner recesses of her surviving self, the place that had always provided a safe haven when her immediate surroundings were no longer where she wanted to be. Ultimately, she had chosen to abandon the city of her birth for a new start in Dhaka, a change that was somehow far less frightening than the prospect of remaining trapped in her existing circumstances forever.

It was the only way of escaping from the endless questions—the orders, rebukes, and demands that had defined her childhood and adolescence. Her father had ruled their lives with impunity, her mother reduced to a pale reflection of the man she had married. Ma had been a young entrant to matrimony, still in her teens when she was handed over like a parcel—carefully wrapped, of course—to a man much older than herself. She had learned her place early, and stayed in it. Although Laila didn't doubt that her father would have made Ma pay dearly had she betrayed any inclination to rebel.

At any rate, Ma never intervened to save her daughters, even on the rare occasions when her husband's anger took on physical dimensions. Perhaps she was incapable of it. Once she was old enough to analyse Ma's behaviour, it had always seemed to Laila that she was too busy just trying to survive the burden that was life.

As it was, Ma had paid a high price for producing two daughters, persisting through several miscarriages until the severe haemorrhaging that followed Laila's birth finally released her from that particular cycle of suffering. But Baba and Ma's relationship had defined for Laila with chilling clarity what she would *not* allow her life to become.

Artistic by nature, her creativity was something that her parents viewed with distrust. Her father, in particular, was adamant in refusing her the pursuit of those interests. Art classes were out of the question, and a series of hidden sketchbooks bore a mute testimony to the lonely passion that refused to die. But Baba knew his stubborn younger child better than to think that matters would end with his refusal regarding the classes. He remained suspicious. Until finally, yet another round of Ma's surreptitious rifling through Laila's clothes cupboard yielded the forbidden materials.

Arriving home in the afternoon, Laila found her parents waiting in her room. Her sense of outrage arrested somewhere between her chest and her throat, she struggled not to react. The pile of sketchpads lay scattered on her writing desk in a way that made her fingers itch to stack them more tidily, even if she could not actually whisk them away to safety. Baba's nostrils flared, his voice tight, as he demanded an explanation—'What do you have to say for yourself, Laila?'

Ma stood silently on one side of the room. She was less an accomplice than a bit player in this drama. Her mind racing to come up a strategic response, Laila decided that passive acceptance of whatever punishment was forthcoming would be the best way to deal with the situation. She kept her eyes trained firmly on the old-fashioned stone floor, with its grey and white geometric patterns, 'I'm sorry, Baba...'

He didn't let her finish. 'Liar—you aren't sorry at all! You've been sneaking around behind my back after I expressly told you to stop all this nonsense! Well, I have had enough of this, enough of your stubbornness and disobedience...' He flung out his arm, sending a few of the pads flying onto the floor. 'Pick those up, and come with me!'

Puzzled, Laila did as she was told, following her father out onto the verandah attached to her bedroom. Shaheen was sitting outside, writing something in a notebook. It was typical of her sister to be doing homework on such a beautiful winter afternoon, instead of relaxing in the garden or reading a book, Laila couldn't help thinking for a brief moment. Sensing the tension that thickened the air, Shaheen slipped the notebook back into her schoolbag, remaining seated.

'Put them down here,' Baba ordered, and Laila complied, reluctantly setting the precious sketchbooks onto the floor, this time in a tidy stack. She didn't realise what he had in mind until Baba took out his lighter. Shaheen's eyes widened in horror, but she remained still.

Not Laila. 'No, Baba! Please...Don't do that!' she begged, even as the small voice in her head pointed out that trying to stop him would just inflame the situation. It always did.

'Are you now telling *me* what to do?' Baba snarled. 'This has gone far enough! How dare you disobey me like this? I will not tolerate such insolence from a daughter of mine! '

'You can't destroy them, Baba—they don't belong to you! *I* don't belong to you!' Laila cried. Even as the words burst out of her mouth, she heard her mother gasp in horror, and knew that she had gone too far.

Laila's defiance inflamed Baba further. If her initial disobedience had not been bad enough, her refusal to recant made matters worse—reinforcing his conviction that girls, whatever their age, should not travel the dangerously seductive route of making their own decisions.

The inevitable flare-up of a temper that was unused to resistance in any form ended in a literal conflagration. The loss of her beloved portfolio was a blow that stung far harder than the slap that accompanied it. Reliving the incident still left Laila shaking with a bitter, pungent anger.

Her sister Shaheen, nine years older, had never had the same difficulties with their parents, perhaps because she was the personification of what their father expected in a daughter, the qualities he considered desirable in a woman. Beautiful, intelligent, and talented she undoubtedly was. But above all, she was docile.

After the bonfire on the verandah, Shaheen had come to Laila's room. But the younger girl was in no mood for sisterly wisdom. 'You know, you shouldn't have had those sketches in your room. Baba told you not to do any more art. He was bound to be angry! Why didn't you just...'

'Leave me alone! I don't need your advice on how to be a good little girl for Baba. One of those in the house is enough' Laila lashed out. Looking hurt, Shaheen was about to continue, when Laila got up, shoved her out of the room and locked the door. If her reaction was too harsh, it felt undeniably good to show her anger to someone without having to worry about the consequences. Nothing her sister could say was likely to help her anyway, she told herself; Laila was no Shaheen.

Even her sister's marriage had been decided by Baba and

Ma, carefully arranged with the scion of a family belonging to the upper echelons of status-conscious Chittagong. The impeccable pedigree of this young *rajputtur* was chosen to provide consolation to a household deprived of a male heir responsible for carrying on the glorious family name.

Perhaps it had been wise to leave the decision to Baba and Ma, Laila thought cynically. At least when her husband unceremoniously abandoned the marriage, her parents couldn't blame Shaheen for making a bad choice.

Laila, on the other hand, was determined to make all her own choices, particularly the bad ones. What had started out as an academic compromise proved to be a fulfilling career after she won an architectural scholarship to a private university in Dhaka. That was an offer that even her father couldn't turn down, although they had few friends and fewer relatives in the capital. It was to be a blessing for Laila, finally free of the suffocating oversight and obsessive interrogations that had characterised her relationship with her parents.

Despite that—and as if to disprove the doomsday mutterings of conservative relatives who maintained that nothing good could ever come of letting a teenage girl go off on her own like that—no major rebellion followed. Laila was too busy keeping her head down and her grades up. She couldn't afford any distractions, nor did she want them. And she allowed herself only female friends, lest rumours of romance filter homewards and pull her back in their wake.

Even with her closest girlfriends, she was careful to distance herself from their wilder shenanigans. The normal pleasures of student life were ruthlessly excluded from her university experience. No, Laila had a plan, and failure just wasn't an option. The parties and boyfriends that many of the other girls took for granted would just have to wait until freedom became a reality to celebrate.

Ironically, once the long-awaited freedom *did* materialise, she was to find that a deep-seated mistrust of men, coupled with an unwillingness to sacrifice her hard-won independence, had created within her a siege mentality where the opposite sex was concerned. That Baba would have approved—for very different reasons—of her capacity for self-protection galled Laila no end.

Ultimately, five years of punishing discipline and single-minded focus paid off, as did the ultimate 'good Bengali girl' lifestyle, even if the latter was essentially meant to ensure that Baba could find no reason to haul her back to Chittagong. Her visits home became progressively more infrequent, heavy work schedules and library access for exam preparations providing a natural (and sufficiently convincing) excuse for her increasing distance from her family.

While some of her friends found her self-sufficiency peculiar, for Laila the logic was simple; trips to her parents' home only reminded her of the unhappiness she had experienced walking the tightrope between her father's impossible standards of behaviour and her own longing to appear 'normal' to her peers at school, most of whom found negotiating the draconian rules that governed Laila's life more trouble than it was worth. Despite the fact that Chittagonians were generally considered to be socially conservative in comparison to those who lived in the more progressive capital, none of Laila's friends had ever been refused permission to attend the annual school picnic on the grounds that it was 'a waste of time, when she should be studying'!

The lure of Western mores of individuality also became

more apparent to her, though she was aware that voicing such opinions would not have been acceptable, especially to her immediate family. So during those ever more widely spaced visits home, she kept her lips pressed together to hold in inappropriate views, and her emotions firmly disengaged.

To her father's probing questions, she provided answers that were as vague as possible. With her sister and nieces, she maintained a friendly but distant manner, the invisible iron fence that surrounded her remaining firmly in place. She smiled and ate the delicacies that her mother painstakingly prepared—luscious tiger prawns swimming in a rich coconut gravy, and the classic *nona ilish*, seasoned fish roe cooked in a mouth-watering lentil and tomato sauce—carefully choosing not to acknowledge the ever-present sadness in those lost, lonely eyes. After all, if Ma needed company, she could always go to her older daughter, who had never left the port city.

And after a few years, Ma didn't even have to go anywhere to visit Shaheen. The family curse had been duly visited on her sister, and after a decade of marriage failed to produce anything more fruitful than two daughters, her husband left abruptly for more promising pastures. Never having had to—or been allowed to—look after herself meant that Shaheen was left completely bereft by this turn of events, and the 'respectability' valued so highly in old-fashioned Chittagong required her to move back to her parental home with her unwanted daughters. At the time, Yasmin had just turned nine, and Aliya was a baby.

But Laila had to give her sister credit. With a meagre BA in impractical English Literature under her belt, Shaheen went back to school, leaving Aliya to be looked after by her grandmother. And within a few years, she had progressed from being a lowly substitute teacher to the coveted post of vice principal at one of the leading English-medium schools in Chittagong. She earned a decent salary, which was just as well, since her ex-husband couldn't be bothered to waste his time or money on his disappointing daughters. But like the good daughter and respectable woman that she was, Shaheen continued to live in her parents' home.

Sometimes Laila wondered what her sister thought about the way her life had turned out. Shaheen had played strictly by the rules, but the outcome of the game had hardly been as expected. She had gone from being an obedient daughter to a dutiful wife, and it now looked as if her last major role would be as a devoted mother. Did she ever wonder who she really was, or what she could have achieved if she had been allowed to make any of the important decisions in life for herself?

Laila had no intention of asking Shaheen any of those questions. What she did know was that she would not be asking anyone for permission to make decisions about her own life. Several job offers had followed her graduation with first-class honours, and her decision to accept a position in a smaller firm established by a recently returned expatriate Bangladeshi ultimately brought her not only greater creative freedom than she might have had with one of the larger, more well-known architectural firms, but also professional recognition. Winning the contract to design the new shopping centre was just the latest in a string of successes for their team.

With the realisation of her cherished dream of financial independence, the last bastion of her father's influence in her life crumbled. Laila had never looked back since. Why would she? There was nothing that she cared to remember about the life she had left behind in Chittagong, least of all the frequent and unflattering comparisons with her sister that had characterised the years she spent there.

But Shaheen's accident changed everything. Laila made an emergency call to her driver, setting out immediately for the city of her birth; waiting for a flight would have meant losing precious hours. What she hadn't bargained for was an interminable return journey with two traumatised children that she barely knew. Shaheen's condition had yet to stabilise, and Laila didn't dare think about what would happen if it didn't.

It was easier to focus on the practical details. There was no way her mother could cope with the long convalescence required for Shaheen's recovery and look after two scared children at the same time. And Baba wasn't likely to be of much help. Between meeting his demands and caring for Shaheen, Ma would be stretched to the limit. So under the circumstances, Laila could not bring herself to refuse to take the children to Dhaka—'just for a few weeks'—however much she might want to. And at least to herself, she could admit that she very much wanted to refuse.

Because they were still on summer break, neither Yasmin nor Aliya would be missing school, and with a live-in housekeeper, Laila already had someone to keep an eye on them during the workday. But having had so little to do with her nieces in the past, she knew that she would have to stretch her creative resources to find ways of keeping them occupied.

She was drawn out of her musings by a sound, realising that Yasmin was awake. Her older niece had been surprisingly accommodating, perhaps to compensate for her little sister's tantrums. Once Aliya fell asleep, Yasmin had occupied herself with the passing landscape of emerald-green rice fields that separated the clusters of thatched mud huts sheltering under a cloudless blue sky.

Some of the homes boasted groves of coconut and betel nut trees, indicating a degree of relative affluence, with a small pond nearby to provide water for bathing, laundry, and washing purposes. Others showed telltale signs of poverty, the roofing of huts gradually wearing away like dandruff flakes departing a scalp, the children standing in front of the houses as scrawny as the goats or the lone cow scavenging for grass and leaves nearby.

Lulled by the picture-perfect rural surroundings and the hypnotic movement of the car, Yasmin soon gave in to her own exhaustion, her even breathing indicating that she had been given a brief respite from her anxieties. As she surveyed the scene outside the car window, Laila could only hope that Yasmin had not taken in the numbers of rusting, skeletal hulks that lay on either side of the highway, reproachfully bearing witness to the recklessness that seemed to afflict so many of the bus drivers in Bangladesh. It was a similar disregard—albeit from the driver of a private car—that had left the girls' mother a splintered mass of flesh and bone cocooned in the fragile comfort of a hospital bed.

'Hi there, awake again?' Laila found herself asking somewhat lamely, hating the artificially upbeat tone of voice she felt compelled to use. Yasmin nodded. Despite her nap, the bruised look around the teenager's eyes indicated that she hadn't had much sleep in the last few days. The protective way she held Aliya as the younger child slept revealed her priorities. If only she had got to know her nieces better before the accident forced them together, Laila thought despairingly, ambushed yet again by an overwhelming sense of inadequacy.

Racking her brain for something intelligent to say, she felt singularly uninspired. Despite acknowledging that it was a pathetic topic to raise with any self-respecting teenager, in an attempt to reach out to Yasmin, Laila found herself resorting to that old conversational standby: school.

'Do you enjoy studying at Dr Khastagir's? It's supposed to be a pretty good school…'

'Yeah, I guess so,' Yasmin answered listlessly.

'Well, I guess it has to be better than studying at a school where your mother is the vice-principal, right?'

'Yes…' This time the response was longer in coming, the teenager's voice sounding thick with suppressed emotion.

Laila could have kicked herself for that accidental reference to Shaheen. The last thing she wanted was to remind Yasmin about her mother's situation. Desperate to change the subject, she continued, 'So what's your favourite among the classes you're taking?'

To her surprise, Yasmin responded with sudden animation to the query. 'It's art, actually. Like you. But I enjoy doing watercolours more than the pencil sketches you did. I think that's what I'm best at.'

Misreading the look of shock on her aunt's face, the teenager continued hurriedly, in a tone of voice clearly meant to pacify her, 'Of course, I do a lot of sketches as well—for portraits, and as outline drawings for my watercolours…' Her words tapered off as she continued to look at Laila, a little uncertain.

'How did you know that I liked sketching?' Laila asked, utterly taken aback by the extent of Yasmin's knowledge about her. There was more to come.

'Ma told me. She said that you were really talented, but *Nana* never allowed you to have art lessons, although you wanted them so badly. He just wanted both of you to study all the time. He's so old-fashioned! There's nothing we can do about that, I guess. It's too late for him to change. But it must have been really difficult for you!

'You know, Ma had the same problem. She had to write her stuff down secretly, in her diaries. She showed me some of them—her stories and poems. She says I can read the rest when I'm older. But I've already seen the story she wrote about you, about the time that *Nana* destroyed your entire portfolio. How could he be so mean! Ma said that you gave up art after that. Is that true? I can't believe you would give up so easily!'

Laila was having trouble absorbing the implications of what Yasmin had so casually revealed, not least the fact that her goody two-shoes sister had ever *had* any secrets. Shaheen's birth had been followed by a series of miscarriages, so it was another decade before Laila finally made her appearance. And as far as she was concerned, quite apart from the age gap, there was a world of difference that separated the two of them.

Growing up, Laila's resentment at Shaheen's effortless ability to live up to their father's idiotic expectations had alienated them from each other. It had never occurred to her that conforming might simply have been her sister's survival strategy. It was unsettling to now consider that they might have had something in common after all.

Unaware of her aunt's thoughts, Yasmin went on, 'I'm so glad that Ma isn't like *Nana*! He thinks it's a waste of time, but she's really proud of my work. So is *Nani*. She keeps one of my pictures in her steel almirah, so that *Nana* won't say anything about it. Actually, I have to say that even *Nana* isn't so bad anymore—at least, not with me. I can't believe he burned your pictures though... Ma said that she had to be even more careful with her diaries after that happened. You must have been so upset!'

'Yes, I was. But you're right, I *did* keep drawing. It's just that after that, I made sure that I never kept any of my sketches at home,' Laila said slowly, struggling to understand how Yasmin could know so much about her. So much more than she herself knew about either of her sister's children. Somehow, thanks to Shaheen's efforts (why had her sister done that—would she ever know?), and despite her own determined distance, Laila had remained a real presence within the family she had so firmly left behind.

Misunderstanding her sudden thoughtfulness, Yasmin continued to chatter. 'At least you're happy now,' she said consolingly. 'It must be great to have a house of your own, and a car, and to be so good at what you do. Everyone in Chittagong talks about how successful you are, and how you've done it all on your own, getting scholarships and everything. And Ma says you didn't even know anyone in Dhaka when you first went there!

'I heard that for a while *Nana* didn't want you to go. *Nani* told me that she thought he was going to say no. Ma says he only allowed you to go because the scholarship was such a big deal, and they couldn't afford to send you to a school like that themselves. But he thought you'd get tired of being alone and decide to come back home anyway. Boy, was he wrong, huh! And now, even *Nani* spends her time showing off to her cousins and the rest of the family about the buildings you've designed.

'You know, I think I might want to be an architect too—if I decide not to be an artist, that is!' Yasmin asserted, laughing. 'Will you show me some of your drawings once we get to Dhaka?'

'Of course,' her aunt responded. 'I'd love to.' Even as she spoke, Laila recognised the truth of what she was saying. Although her colleagues and friends had always been supportive, it would be nice to share something so important to her with someone who was actually part of her family. It opened the door to all kinds of possibilities.

The kindred soul that she sensed in Yasmin made Laila feel a genuine sense of connection with her niece—not least because she knew that they shared a troubled relationship with their fathers. It made Laila wonder what might come out of an honest conversation with her sister, once Shaheen had recovered. *If* she recovered, she thought in sudden terror. She pushed the thought away as quickly as it had popped up.

It remained to be seen whether the chance to have that particular conversation would ever materialise for the two of them, but in the meantime, Laila had an opportunity to get to know the girls properly, especially Yasmin. With uncharacteristic optimism, she allowed herself to fleetingly consider the idea that a *relative* of hers might one day be part of her female inner circle.

Their conversation was interrupted as Aliya awoke, but somehow Laila had no doubt that it would be resumed.

As the little girl rubbed away the clinging remnants of sleep from her eyes, the other two braced themselves for the inevitable barrage of questions that was bound to follow. Yet this time it was different, and Laila smiled reassuringly as she met Yasmin's anxious eyes. Anticipating Aliya's unspoken question, she responded, 'Don't worry, sweetheart. It won't take much longer, I promise. We're getting there...'

Wax Doll

ABEER HOQUE

a drop of wax is born
it slowly gathers
weight, fullness
until the moment
it is roundest
then motion
a liquid interior
breaks through the skin
comes forth
slides the drop down
inexorably down
till it disappears

Ila was sitting in her father's dining room, surrounded by the remains of dinner. The heat of the summer was as liquid a presence as rain, though it hadn't rained during the day. Her t-shirt was dark with sweat, but she was determined not to switch on the air conditioner. It was her new rule because she hated the transition from dry, cold AC air into

An earlier version of this story appeared in the *Daily Star* newspaper (Bangladesh) on 24 May 2008.

real Dhaka. It was like a paradigm shift, and it wilted her. Like a *momer putul*, a little wax doll, her *Nana* would say fondly. Without the AC, Ila was only half listless all the time, instead of bouncing between two extremes. Still, she insisted on the heat, even as her spiked-up hair got less edgy by the hour.

'The last thing anyone should want nowadays,' her mother was saying, 'is a love marriage.'

Her father retorted, 'No one does arranged marriages anymore. Not unless there's a mullah in the immediate family. That's certainly not ours.' He swirled his glass of wine meaningfully and winked at Ila.

Ila found herself silently agreeing with her mother. She knew what havoc love could wreak. Her own parents had been estranged her entire life, despite a beginning that boasted of true love. Many people had told Ila that her parents had been considered *the* example of a love marriage. Nita and Seku's affectionate and humorous exchanges were still remembered decades later. One story took place at a wedding, before Ila was born. Her mother's fury at her father's late arrival had turned into helpless laughter when he appeared with two large, blooming irises. With a solemn face, he first affixed one flower behind his ear, and then with exaggerated care placed the other behind hers. Others spoke of how their every encounter began and ended with a kiss.

Ila couldn't quite see her decorous father kissing anyone in public. And she didn't remember her parents not fighting, or worse, renouncing fighting for a louder sort of silence. Her mother first started leaving her father when Ila was a baby, in an increasing whirlwind of business trips, with each one taking her farther away for longer periods. Her father countered by having an affair with Modhu Aunty, the wife of his best friend, capping another love marriage gone wrong.

When her mother emigrated to America, she took Ila with her, leaving her father heartbroken and alone. Ila could see the years on his face, still elegant but lined and gaunt. It was the only reason she had stopped kicking and screaming. When her mother pulled her out just before her last year of high school in America, dragging her back to Bangladesh, she felt as if she had died, or arrived on another planet. Once Ila realised that her mother wasn't going to budge, she set herself to finding her Dhaka groove. Her father's unrestrained joy at their return was her first and favourite track.

'Did you hear Modhu's daughter has divorced her husband?' her mother exclaimed. 'They got married a few months back.'

Ila's father looked shocked, but said nothing. Ila didn't know if it was the mention of Modhu Aunty, or her daughter's split.

'The guy was gross!' Ila said, more to deflect the conversation than anything. 'I don't know what Shurobhi saw in him.'

'She was in love,' said her mother. 'You know, that virus infecting everyone these days.'

'What I don't get is why she looked so sad even at the wedding. It's like the old days, when brides had to look in mirrors and cry their eyes out.'

'Or maybe it was the weight of seven sets of jewellery,' her mother said, pressing her ample cleavage as if weighed down herself. 'Modhu always did overdo it on the plumage, so it's only natural that her daughter would too.'

This time even Ila flinched, and her mother finally stopped

her tirade. She knew her mother was not being herself.
Ordinarily light-hearted and funny, even silly, she turned
brittle and hard around Ila's father. These weekly dinners
were a strain and Ila wished her mother would stop trying,
just let Ila eat with each of them separately, in peace.

But now Ila was afraid of other things, afraid for all
the rose-blinded couples, unable to see the love-propelled
disaster descending, afraid for her own chances at marital
joy. She wasn't going to get married just to get divorced. She
knew how hard it was, even when you loved someone to
pieces. She was going to be prepared.

Ila met the jilting bride in question a few weeks later at a
garden party. Shurobhi was decked out lavishly, as befitted
a newly-wed, but with none of the attendant diffidence.
Chain smoking through a pack of Bensons, she ignored all
the whispering aunties and invited Ila to sit with her.

'Should we talk about my divorce and get it over with?'
Shurobhi said, arching her pencil-thin eyebrows.

Ila laughed, winding her sari *anchal* around her shoulders
to keep the mosquitoes at bay. 'Only if you want to. Because
I think I already have the scoop, just from walking through
the garden of gossip.'

'OK, fine. I know divorces can ruin you, especially if
you're a woman,' Shurobhi said wryly, 'but at least it means
you're not trapped for the rest of your life.'

'True,' Ila replied carefully. She didn't want to offend
Shurobhi, but she had her own take on this from her
experience as a child of divorced parents. She continued, 'But
in the old days, you had to fight tooth and nail to get into
a love marriage, and it usually lost you everything else. So
you'd have to really want someone to go to all that trouble,

choose carefully. And God forbid you picked poorly, because after all the hassle, who'd want to walk away? Who could?'

'So what's your point? People aren't choosing carefully now?'

'Yes! Because it's so much easier now to find love. People pick carelessly and then—compounding the problem—they try less. Maybe they think the love bit will take care of the rest. But it won't.'

'And the solution is you let someone else choose your husband for you? But who chooses? Your divorced parents?' Shurobhi asked pointedly.

'Good point. I'm not sure, actually,' Ila admitted. 'Anyway, I'll vet my beaus a little bit. I'm just saying I'm not going to look too closely, especially after the *akth*. Once the engagement is done, there's no going back. I'm going to make do with my lot. Make it happen the old-fashioned way. The way it worked for my grandparents and their grandparents.'

'OK, you turn your blind eye. I'm going to check back with you in ten years when you're stuck with some *phorsha* fool.' The edge in Shurobhi's voice was softened by what sounded like pity.

Ila smiled even as she shook her head. She was going to make her own marriage work, through quips or quiescence, one way or another. Prayers by a paynim. After all, Ila still performed the *Maghreb* prayer. It was the only one she did now, though she used to do all five when she was younger, when her mother left, when her father was left behind. When she thought it might bring them back together. She only prayed this last one now because she was unwilling to totally give up hope, in either God or her parents.

'Come over sometime, Shurobhi,' Ila said, finding herself genuinely wanting Shurobhi to do that. 'In fact, come next Saturday to my dad's flat in Gulshan. My best friend, Rox, is visiting from America. You can meet her. She's a riot.'

Shurobhi smiled, tipping her lipstick-stained cigarette from bejewelled fingers. 'That'd be nice.'

When Shurobhi came over for lunch, Ila and Rox were already drunk. Ila poured out an opaque tumbler of her father's wine and handed it over to Shurobhi jauntily.

'Ila, your hair looks good long,' Rox exclaimed. 'I can't remember the last time you grew it out.'

'I'm glad you mentioned that,' Shurobhi said, 'because I was wondering what the deal was with the American punk 'do.' She drawled out the word American.

Ila laughed, wringing her hair like a mop and releasing it. 'I'm just trying to play the good Bangladeshi girl. You know, so I can land a good Bangladeshi boy.'

'Forget it. There's none out there,' Shurobhi said.

'Not one?' asked Rox in disappointment. 'What about that boy whose photos your mom showed us? He looks cute.'

'Tahsin. Yeah, my mother loves his parents, and him,' said Ila with a twist of her mouth. 'We stayed with his family when we first moved back to Bangladesh.'

'I've known Tahsin since we were kids,' Shurobhi said, amused. 'You like him, Ila?'

'I've only talked to him a few times.' Ila found herself embarrassed without knowing why.

To change the subject, she picked up the newspaper sports page and intoned heavily, 'Oh... oh, it was not easy for the skipper to—ACCEPT—the fact that he was no longer... *captain*.' She whispered the last word.

Rox started to shake with silent laughter. It was one of their oldest forms of entertainment, Ila's naturally hoarse voice at once mimicry, seduction, and melodrama. And the Bangladeshi sports page displayed a kind of emotion and exuberance that was perfect for this purpose.

'What shocked me most was the way I was treated!' Ila switched to a high-pitched socialite's whine, and jumped up, pressing her hands against her heart. She pranced up the dining room, her *dupatta* trailing behind her, hair syncopating with her motion. When she turned, both Rox and Shurobhi were watching her intently. Her heart lurched with the same lost feeling she'd had before leaving America. Dropping to her knees before Rox, Ila told her one version of the truth.

'I pitch before you, skipper mine.' Her hands cupped Rox's shoulders. 'My 'wicket' heart has no chance against you. Give us a kiss.'

Rox obliged. She leaned down and pressed her lips against Ila's.

Ila was the first to break away, pounding heart, ribboned breath.

'Lovely,' Shurobhi said, clapping. 'Let's have another glass of Seku Uncle's wine and then we can go see your future husband.'

'What? Who?' Ila said, feeling paper thin and transparent.

'Tahsin. He's having a party at his place, except of course they call it an orgy.'

'An orgy?' Ila said, feeling even denser.

'Don't worry, they're not really,' Shurobhi said, lighting a cigarette. 'I mean there's drinking, smoking, even hooking up. But not like sex or anything. More's the pity. But come on.'

The rain was coming down, pressing the failing heat

aside. The air sailed between tranquility and tumult, as the three banged out of the sprawling flat. The front door was a Balinese gem that her mother had brought back on one of her trips. It writhed with animal carvings that made Ila feel that the door was alive. Her father kept large leafy plants on either side of the entrance, making the illusion of jungle-pounce even more potent.

They skipped down the marbelised stairs, into the rising wind. Rox and Ila were holding hands, half running, half screaming, as the rain made its first sweep, spattering Ila's grey *kameez* black. Halfway down the next street, cowering under an obscenely pregnant jackfruit tree, Rox and even the normally reserved Shurobhi couldn't stop laughing.

'Ila, I don't know what it is about you,' Shurobhi said, lighting a cigarette as the wind pulled the rain down and about. 'Your hair, your face, your ability to get wet in a second, but you are straight out of a Bollywood film.'

Ila looked at herself. Her ordinary *kameez* and fine lace *dupatta* had become a dark mould of her curvy body. Her hair, usually a surging mass around her shoulders, lay in thick parsed strands plastered around her face. She pushed a strand aside self-consciously, aware she was only unreeling the scene.

'No wonder the boys all want,' Shurobhi exhaled the words through the smoke.

Ila opened her mouth to protest, and Rox put a finger on her lips, shushing her. 'You only have to speak with that melty wax-doll voice of yours, and we'll all be goners. *Cholo*. Let's go.'

They resumed their push-pull stumbling run through the rain. At Tahsin's mansion of a house, Shurobhi kicked off

her sandals into a pile of shoes in the foyer and ascended the
gleaming granite stairs. Rox followed, as Ila prised her shoes
off more slowly, stepping on their curled toes and letting them
spring back. She looked up to see an older woman, the maid
who had opened the door, standing there watching her.

'How are you, Komola?' she asked, remembering her
name at the last second. The last time she had seen Komola
was after Ila's mother had whisked Ila away from America
back to Bangladesh. Ila hadn't realised her mother was
serious about coming back in the beginning, even when
she had gone to Dhaka on her own first to find a flat for
them. It was only when she came back to Baltimore to get Ila
that it had sunk in. The flat hadn't been ready, so they lived
in Tahsin's bougainvillea-draped house for a few months.
Much to Tahsin's mother's amazement, in that short time,
Ila's mother had struck up a friendship with the old maid,
Tahsin's beloved nanny, Komola.

When they arrived from the airport, Komala and Ila's
mother greeted each other like old friends, laughing and
hugging. But then, when Ila and her mother were alone in
the bedroom, Komola came in weeping. They tried to comfort
her, but the maid was inconsolable. Ila didn't understand
much of the garbled story that came pouring out. It was
about Komola's husband, a love marriage it seemed. But
there was something about his strange eyes, and another
wife. A contract made, a contract broken. And Ila guessed
this last part: finding love, and then losing it. Ila thought
perhaps it had never been there to begin with. Not real love
anyway, the kind that made you stay, no matter what.

Komola shrugged tiredly. 'I'm here, as I've always been.'

Ila had no response. What could she say in the face

of such exhaustion? She squeezed Komola's arm. It was unexpectedly soft.

Komola patted her back, and then said in a brighter voice, 'But my sister, July, has returned, by the grace of God! From India, though I did not even know where she had been all these years. I thought I would never see her again, but God had other plans. We cannot know what is written on our foreheads. We must not know, or else we would not be able to bear it! Life is very long.'

Ila was lost in thought as she ascended the stairs. The floor felt cool under her wet feet. She stopped outside Tahsin's room, from which raucous voices were filtering out through the half-open door. She could hear Shurobhi introducing Rox around. When she went in, Ila saw people lounging on Tahsin's enormous bed and on the rug that lay on the floor, lined with pillows. Most of the faces were familiar, but there was a boy she didn't recognise leaning against the far wall. He was older than the rest of them and wearing a rain-stained *kurta*. She remembered her own clothes drenched against her body and pulled at her *kameez* uncomfortably. When she looked up again, she saw him watching her. Before she could respond, something passed between them. It had nothing to do with words, not even with feelings, but a kind of understanding.

She took a deep breath and pushed open the door. A pop tarantella was playing on the Bose speakers. The room fell silent and before anyone could greet her, she put a finger to her lips dramatically. Snapping her fingers in time, she glided into the room in a spurious version of the tango, her arms akimbo. She paused near Rox and vogued. Rox whooped, taking on the snapping rhythm.

'Are you ready for it?' Ila asked the room huskily. Voices chimed in assent. She noticed Tahsin draped over a chair by the stereo, inhaling from a joint, his chiselled face engaged. Ila clapped her hands down on her thighs and proceeded to smack different parts of her body.

'Is it the Macarena?' someone called out as Ila kicked one leg out and then another, at odd, hooked angles. Rox jumped up beside Ila and followed her lead, fumblingly.

'No, it's the *makorsha*!' Ila spiked her clawed hands in the air, spider-like.

Water drops flung themselves from her swinging hair. Her backup dancer collapsed, laughing. Ila couldn't look in the stranger's direction for fear she'd fly apart. She didn't know why. She couldn't look at Rox either. So she looked at Tahsin, who hadn't stopped watching her since she had entered the room.

'Ila,' he said. 'How do you come up with the shit you do? It's hysterical.'

She shrugged, smiling, and sat down beside Shurobhi. A dance party had started up. The tarantella transitioned into an electronically remixed Baul song.

'If nothing else, Tahsin has a stellar music collection,' Shurobhi whispered in her ear.

It was true, but not quite fair, Ila thought. Tahsin had much more than a hard drive full of eclectic MP3s. He also had a witty tongue, generous habits, and an unfailing charm with women. Which included every female, from his terrorising grandmother to Komola, his overprotective ayah of twenty years.

The sun was burning its way through the rain clouds, though the air-conditioned house didn't give a hint of the heat. Rox was still gyrating to the music, and had pulled others into her orbit, including the stranger. He was older than Ila had first thought, maybe in his thirties, or even older. His eyelids were dark and his frame too thin. But she liked the lines around his eyes, his clinging kurta, his pricking presence. Someone flashed a million-watt smile at him, and Ila felt a clawing in her chest.

'He's an artist,' Shurobhi said into her ear.

'Who?' she said carelessly, though she knew perfectly well.

'Oyon, Tahsin's older brother. Has the best yabba hookups. Crazy, too.'

The stranger was next to her now, his bent of body inviting hers. She stilled herself to stone. She had always had trouble staying inside herself. In the time that followed, she became acutely conscious of every movement in both their bodies, within the room. Her skin prickled with every lean-in, each brush-past, all intimated offerings. The hair on her neck stood up and she struggled to control her breathing, her heart.

The stranger traced a lank piece of Ila's hair. She was unable to keep herself together. When he took her arm, Ila barely felt his touch. Or she felt it too much. Her legs dissolved into the charged air, yet somehow she found herself standing by him, now dancing. He stood behind her, his arms lengthening along hers. Rox swayed in front of her, her palm pressing the damp flatness of Ila's stomach, her face achingly close.

Ila wanted to know if it were possible to want two opposite things at once, passion and reason, each growing fruit and fruit-eating serpents in her garden. Even before the game started, there were so many ways to lose. She wanted to remain in the moment, wanted the moment to last, wanted to remember forever what this felt like, to stand between the old and the new, both urgent, neither tenable.

As the music segued again, this time to a trance samba number, the stranger moved away. Ila knew the moment was lost, no one else's but hers to recall. Her legs took shape, her arms grew heavy at her sides, her skin condensed back onto her body, blood rush by blood rush. She stood in the centre of the room, coming together at the seams.

The next time Shurobhi came over, Ila's father's flat was a bustle of activity.

'What's going on?'

'My mother's coming over soon, with my aunt. They're taking me to a bride viewing.'

'Who's the bride?'

'Me.'

Shurobhi's posture turned rigid. 'What? You've agreed to this?'

'Well, it's only a preliminary meeting,' she replied. 'You know the one where you go to be inspected by your teeth-gnashing mother-in-law, who will say you're too fat and dark, but she supposes she could train you into a decent housewife type.'

'Is this a joke?'

'No,' Ila said, smiling. 'And I'm actually looking forward to it.'

Shurobhi stared at her, unable to say more.

Ila went on, 'I'll tell you what I know. He has a Masters degree and a job in America. And his parents are worried because he's close to thirty and still unmarried.'

'Tall and fair too, I'm sure,' Shurobhi said, her lips twisting.

'Hard to tell from the photos, but promising... And Tahsin is next on the bio data list, though I kind of wish it were his brother. Come, check out my outfit.' Ila was determined not to let Shurobhi get her down. So she couldn't tell her that what she really wanted was for time to just stop, so that she could stay where nothing had been decided, everything was to come, for better or for worse.

It was only in the car heading to Dhanmondi that Ila thought about how she might appear to Rox or Shurobhi, or any of their friends. They would find it absurd, even though these days parental introductions followed by a period of dating were not uncommon. It was just the method of introduction that stood out here, replete with stiff families in starched outfits and arch commentary.

An hour and a half later, the five of them were still in the car, the traffic more jammed than usual. The driver and her mother were silent. Her aunt kept up a running monologue, which Ila had thought was relieving at first but now found tiresome. Her father fidgeted in the front passenger seat. He interrupted his sister-in-law, his British accent clipping off the edges of his sentences. 'The house is on Road Eight, no? Shouldn't have come this way. Now we're late. Looks bad.'

'It's fine,' said her aunt. 'We get to be fashionably late. And they must understand the traffic situation. They live in this neighbourhood, after all.' She eyed the immobile snake of cars with distaste.

Ila refrained from reminding her aunt that she herself had lived in this neighbourhood not too long ago. She twisted her crushed silk *dupatta* in her hands. Good thing she had

picked a *shalwar kameez* with forgiving fabric for the car ride.
Of course, her aunt had disapproved of the colour, saying the
cerise was too dark for Ila's skin tone, but Shurobhi insisted
it looked good. Ila thought so too.

Outside, the street traffic thrummed and throbbed. School
had let out, and streams of laughing, blue-pinafored girls
were weaving between the cars. Braids of varying lengths
and messiness swung past her window. She wished she were
in high school again, when things weren't so complicated,
when she was surer of what made sense. All the certainty
arising from her conversations with Shurobhi faded. If
there wasn't love to begin with, then she had to count on it
creating itself out of nothing. Could something like that see
her through the rest of her life? Could it be deep enough,
wide enough to contain her ridiculous, hopeful heart?

What if it weren't? What if they had children? At that
time, would it matter if she had gone into it for love or for
reason? Did she really know anything about how the world
worked, what it required? Were all the movies and the books
so wrong about that missing piece—the love bit—that made
you want to be part of the greater whirl, that seemed to solve
everything in the beginning, but that Ila knew wouldn't
solve anything in the end?

Why, she asked God silently, is it so hard to understand
how to be happy?

By the time Ila walked into the flat on Road Eight, she
was ready for anyone who showed even a trace of certainty.
Soon enough, she was enveloped by it. Her voluble aunt,
his plainspoken mother, her sharp-tongued *Nana* who had
insisted on taking a rickshaw on his own to meet them. Even
the would-be groom, though he said little, seemed assured

in his reserve. His eyes were direct, his lips full, his hands folded in his lap. She felt all their gazes pulling at her, digging holes, leaving her diluted, a collection of parts that didn't quite add up to a whole.

Only her father seemed unsure, and Ila found herself gravitating to him. Now, all the confidence seemed suspect, brimming the room with hot air, making it difficult to think. She needed to leave and when she looked at her father, he knew this immediately. The meeting was brought to a close, a second one planned with an enthusiasm Ila found difficult to believe. How did the dour logistics of the conversation fade? Had the advent of parting sugarcoated the thought of their next connection?

She was startled when the boy appeared in front of her. Her *Nana* raised his voice in an attempt to create the illusion of privacy. She found it absurd and touching.

'Let's go for coffee soon,' he said. Ila could only nod. 'Could I have your mobile number?'

Ila fumbled for her phone and when she finally retrieved it, she stared at it blankly. He took the phone from her hand and started entering his number. She was both piqued and relieved by his gesture, but said nothing. He gave it back to her, gently vibrating.

'Missed call from you to me,' he said, smiling easily, waving his own phone. 'I-L-A... is that right?' His tongue seemed to be testing the letters.

She watched his lips move in slow motion. She could do this, she thought, come to know that mouth, those hands, discover a different arrangement of her heart, one where you knew the end wasn't in sight every beating moment.

'Yes,' she said at last. 'That's right.'

Over and Over Again

Tisa Muhaddes

Despair reigned. Anju's frail body lay cocooned in a sheath of soft cotton. Perched on the bed, I surveyed the room like an eagle scouting the lay of the land. I wanted to cry, but my voice lay smothered in the embers of unspoken thoughts. I was mute but alert.

The caravan of women—the older ones shrouded in white—floated through the rooms, commiserating in hushed tones. 'What a tragedy,' they whispered. 'How could life be so cruel to such a young girl...?'

'It wasn't accidental—they say she was pushed!' exclaimed others. 'She was so beautiful...How could she have fallen from the roof like that—and when there were other people around, too,' they continued.

'What misfortune! Look at her catatonic father curled up in a corner in the bedroom. Look at her mother pleading desperately for the return of her child,' the women said. 'What a dreadful tragedy!'

I was six when he started. It was never in a dark room. Shards of memory are my only proof. They rear their heads from the depths of an abysmal darkness, pricking and piercing me mercilessly with their truth. I see and comprehend with a clarity that shields my shame. Random scenes unfold like parts of a film that I cannot piece together, yet am forced to replay over and over again in my mind.

I remember my pigtails bobbing up and down, my plaid dress brushing against my body as I hurried to catch the events that were causing such a commotion. 'Oh, oh, oh,' I thought. 'I must see why the children are shouting outside.' His bedroom opened out into the biggest and longest balcony overlooking our courtyard. One could stand there and glimpse the outer boundaries of our neighbourhood.

The neighbourhood then was bordered by lush, vivid foliage that shimmered and shimmied under the adoring gaze of the sun. Block-shaped white buildings rose up from the earth to complement nature's verdant greenery. Our house was the oldest in the area, our property the largest, our family the first settlers on this once-fallow land.

I exploded through the doors, oblivious to his presence in the bedroom, and made a beeline for the balcony door. It was locked and I crashed headlong into it. He laughed as he saw me rub my forehead, wincing and befuddled. He materialised from the bathroom, adjusting his pajamas, and with one swift movement scooped me up to his chest.

I wriggled and squirmed as he admonished me to be careful. 'Open the door! Oh, open the door!' I pleaded. Laughing, he gently planted me on the floor, and unhinged the locks. Once my feet touched solid ground, I plunged forward onto the balcony, fearing that the commotion had dissipated just as I arrived. But it hadn't.

Someone had dropped a brick from our rooftop and it had landed on the brand-new car that Sajid *Bhaiya,* the local heartthrob, had bought just the day before. It was prominently parked in our courtyard, basking shamelessly in the sunlight which gilded its lustrous silver body. Now the windshield was broken, a huge gash ran along its body, hundreds of little cracks branching out from the scar like small crooked fangs.

The brick lay on top—shattered, exposed, and shamed. The culprit had absconded. Sajid *Bhaiya* stood silently next to his car, disbelief and outrage emanating from his every pore. His mother stood slightly apart, screaming at the crowd that had gathered. She was shouting obscenities and cursing over and over again.

I leaned against the wall of the balcony, teetering on my tiptoes, brimming with unbridled excitement. What would happen next? Who was responsible? Would Sheila Aunty beat someone? Would Sajid *Bhaiya* speak?

I heard my name, softly whispered behind me. I turned back, expecting him to conspiratorially wink at me, relishing another's misfortune. But he didn't wink. He was staring at me. Oddly. A sudden coldness seized my body. I took a step back, unconsciously creating distance between us. He abruptly walked back into his bedroom. I returned to the commotion outside…

…He had me pinned against the bed. I looked at him, but his face was a blur. I could smell his warm sticky breath as he whispered my name, nuzzling my ears. His free hand was roaming, meandering its insistent way over my sullied skin. He gently lowered his body on top of mine…. I looked at the locked door…. He placed a hand gently over my mouth and whispered '*Eita shudhu ador*… this is only affection' over and over again…

I heard my ayah calling my name outside his door, the

panic swelling in her voice. He emerged from the bathroom and yelled to give him a minute. He walked over to where I was lying naked, trying not to stare at the small puddle of milky liquid gathered in the folds of the bed sheet. Speaking in a soothing voice, he put my clothes on me one at a time, gently repeating '...*eita shudhu ador*... this is only affection...'

When he opened the door, my ayah almost tripped in her hurry to pick me up in her arms. She immediately started chastising me for disappearing. Then she apologised for disturbing *Choto Sahib*. She demanded I say sorry to *Choto Chacha* for ruining his afternoon nap. She assured him she wouldn't lose sight of me again. She noticed the crumpled bed, the milky puddle, and my frozen state. She didn't say a word.

I cannot remember other episodes, or even if there were any more. But his stench, his kisses on my shoulders, on my chest, on my arms, on my legs, in my secret crevices—those I cannot clean away.

As I sat quietly in a corner of that room, its aura pregnant with misfortune, I sighed with a relief that seemed twenty years too late. I spied *Choto Chacha* in his daughter's adjoining room, clutching a framed picture of Anju on her ninth birthday, attempting to fathom the injustice of his loss.

All it took was a simple push to make the world all right again. Curling and uncurling my aching fingers, I remained still in the corner, staring at Anju's body, whispering silently, 'It wasn't my fault, it wasn't my fault' over and over again.

Touch Me Not

S. BARI

Ma made him buy boots before he left. 'They're very expensive over there.' They keep his feet warm and dry, these ankle-high lace-up boots, but he dreads putting them on, even as his second cold winter glides into town. He fights his feet in, wiggling until the heels drop into place, and feels he has tied weights around his ankles. He spent his childhood and adolescence in rubber flip-flops and canvas 'keds' and the occasional black loafers. He hurries to class, dragging these boots through the carpet of dry snow.

When he first arrived, he relished the chill autumn, the sharp crack of dry leaves, and the colours along the tree tops—yellow, mustard, gold, saffron, vermilion, fawn—stretched out like saris drying in the sun. He signed up at student housing and picked out his classes, chatted with anyone he wished, and ate whatever he craved. But now, as the days darken and the trees bare their branches, the spaciousness of solitude gives way to the claustrophobia of loneliness.

He is a small-town boy, and he has come to study for a graduate degree in another small town, through the looking glass and across the world. For his first Thanksgiving, a local family invites him home. He diligently swallows the bland turkey meat and helps with the washing up. He calls his parents regularly, using pre-paid discount cards bought at the corner store.

'Tonight I'm going to a political event. The town is going to elect a mayor, and my friends have asked me to help fold letters.'

He knows nothing about the candidates and isn't interested, but he wants to see how these things work here. The room is in the back of the library, with very bright lights and a long vinyl-topped table covered with sheets of paper. Music is blaring from the loudspeakers, and volunteers are shouting to each other. He feels at home in the organised raucousness. Someone hands him a letter and shows him the required fold. He follows suit, folding once, then twice, till every letter is perfectly folded in three. When the folding is done, he is handed a large brown box and a cutter.

'Posters of the candidate. Give everyone fifty each to put up around town.'

Slicing into the masking tape and folding back the cardboard, he sees her picture. 'Deborah Smith for Mayor'. Her black hair, cut short now. Her chin is rounder and her jaw at once fuller and sharper. She is looking at the camera straight on, wearing something red. There are little gold earrings in her ears. Her hesitant smile is just the same.

He was ten when she came to his small town. She had signed up for Volunteer Away right after college, and when they assigned her a country, she ran home and looked for 'her' country in the atlas. There it was, wedged like a plug between India and Burma, spreading into the brown waters of the Bay of Bengal. 'More like fingers of land than an entire solid country,' she told him.

The whole family went to receive her at the train station. She was the only white person who got off the train. His parents had made him wear his best pair of trousers and a scratchy shirt with a collar. He expected a woman with blonde hair, wearing short clothes and showing the tops of her breasts like the white women in the posters his cousin hid under the mattress. But she came out wearing a *shalwar kameez* that someone had bought her in the capital, and her hair was long and black like his mother's. As she came towards them, he saw her eyes were blue.

Ma hugged her and told her she was welcome in their town and in their home. *Baba* held out his hand for her suitcase. And then she looked down at the ten-year old boy.

'Who's this?'

'My name is Aleem.'

He was speaking English to a native-born English speaker for the first time in his life. She knew not to say more—he couldn't answer more. She walked with him to the car that *Baba* had borrowed from Uncle for this trip.

He wondered how she knew what to do, how to eat with the fingers of her right hand, and how to cover her head with her veil at the right times. Who had told her these things? *Ma* said she was respectful and kind. In the morning, he walked with her to the girls' school, where she stopped at the gate and turned to say goodbye, while he walked on to the boys' school. Her *shalwar* was short on her, and her ankles showed. She walked like a boy. She taught English to the big girls.

'What's in here?' She turned over the little packet of twisted clear plastic wrap stuffed with dark-brown paste.

They stood at the candy-man's cart in front of the girls' school. Fluorescent tubes of chewing gum and chocolate in bright red wrappers lay stacked next to crackling bags of roasted chickpeas. He bit a corner of the packet and squeezed the paste out, grimacing as the sour shock of it hit his tongue.

'*Tetul.*'

What was it in English? They decided to stop by the market and ask the man who sold old paper for re-use and recycling. He was known to understand several languages.

'Tamarind,' he told them definitively, frowning at the two of them. 'Why do you want to know?'

She held up the plastic sleeve of tamarind paste and giggled, and he frowned again.

'You will get sick on that stuff,' his voice came after them.

He sits back on his heels, squatting the way they can't here. He holds the poster and looks carefully again. It *is* her, and she seems well.

The posters are put up in the right neighbourhoods. He becomes a campaign regular. He googles Deborah Smith, reads about her in the free paper in town. She talks about making the town a place that young people want to stay on and work in, even after they graduate. About setting up research facilities and creating jobs, about the need to be welcoming to immigrants because they create ideas and wealth, and about caring for the less fortunate. Her opponent calls her a communist and hints at lesbianism.

He goes to a political rally and sees her standing on a platform that is level with his chin. She has no security, at least none that he can see. She is muffled in a scarf, but the front of her coat is open, so she must be a little warm from the exertion of the speech. He does not remember her words later, but her voice is familiar. The high, light voice of sixteen years ago has not matured or deepened. Instead, from the elegant, coated figure in the scarf and low heels comes the voice of the twenty-three-year-old, fresh-out-of-college girl on her first Volunteer Away assignment.

He and *Baba* sat together at dinner time, their enamelled plates steaming with rice. *Ma* stood by *Baba*'s side, serving the vegetables first—crunchy okra or slimy eggplant, tender potatoes, or his favourite, red spinach that came only in the winter. Then the fish, sometimes prickly with bones, which gradually collected at the side of the plate. Debi watched *Baba* delicately pick out the bones and tried to do the same, but she eventually gave up and just chewed determinedly until they were reduced to a lumpy mass. *Ma* laughed at her and showed her again and again how to pick out each slender filament from the flesh, without success.

Aleem's oldest cousin, who was twenty, asked if he ever saw her breasts. Aleem had not even seen the tops of her breasts, because she never wore saris, only *kameez*, which went up to her neck. But his cousin and he could look at the bras she wore, hanging on the laundry line, even though *Ma* hung them on the line behind the water tank on the roof. They were of a cloth so fine that it seemed transparent to him, and one of them had tiny blue flowers on the bowls where her breasts went.

She helped Aleem with homework, and he helped her learn Bangla. Within a month, she knew how to buy things at the market, to take the laundry to the ironing man and count the pieces of clothing, to be stern with the older boys in the market who followed her, and to name most of the plants in the garden. The whole family went to the village for Eid, and she joined *Ma* for a bath in the river. He knew because they left with several other women, carrying cakes of soap and extra saris. When she came back, *Ma* had wrapped her in a sari, and Aleem saw her shoulders were pink with a small white stripe.

The only desk in the house, apart from his father's, was in the room that they had given their guest. In the evenings, she sat on her bed, reading and writing letters home, while he studied at the desk. 'What is the English for *ilish machh*?'

Her grubby dictionary told them it was *hilsa*. 'Although that's not really an English word, I think,' she would say, rubbing her chin.

They debated why there was no real word for 'thank you' except for the excessively formal *dhonnobad*.

'Everyone knows you're a foreigner when you say that.'

'Everyone knows I'm a foreigner anyway,' she said, and they giggled. It was what the boys in the market called after her, singing about women from faraway lands that they loved. When *Ma* walked with her, they did not dare, but with only Aleem around, they were bolder. Sometimes they followed her down the narrow mud-carpeted lanes, wagging their hips and saying words that Aleem knew he could not translate even if he wanted. Then the stall-keepers would swear at them or cuff one of them on the head.

The campaign group is informal and unfunded. When it comes time to hold fancy fundraising events, the most they can do is wangle a banquet hall from a local restaurateur. But the food must be served, and Aleem and others are brought in, tucked into black suits and bow ties, and handed platters lined with little slices of bread cradling cucumbers, shrimps or asparagus. Trays bristle with tall glasses of sparkling wine. He is nervous with the drinks trays, an incipient wobble always threatening his elbow. Tired velvet curtains sag by the French windows under the slightly bluish lights. Across a small field of white-clothed tables, he sees her walk in.

She is smaller than he remembers. Several organisers gather by her side in a deferential gaggle, keeping a slight but constant distance. 'Here, shall we have a photo op right under the entrance?' 'Can we check out the podium?' Their voices form a bubble around her, moving with her as she glides through the crowd. She shakes hands, smiles, nods or frowns, touches elbows, and looks concerned. He, too, nods and smiles as guests graze snacks off his tray and denude his forest of drinks. He hands out tiny napkins and swings into the kitchen for refills. She is sometimes far from him and sometimes near enough for him to start worrying. What if she recognises him—and remembers what no one would want to remember? What if she doesn't recognise him?

He is being guided by a woman about his own age towards the centre of the room. 'Can we get Ms. Smith some refreshments?'

She smiles the big smile that American women own, inclusive and apparently indiscriminate. She moves him in the direction she wants without touching him. He has to follow.

He holds out the tray and Debi reaches for a drink. 'Thank you.' And looks at him with a smile.

She has not recognised him.

His father's small house was matched by a small garden. While *Ma* tended her dahlias and gardenias, he preferred the hidden huddles of weeds and the tiny pond where he could catch frogs. He showed Debi where the water lilies sheltered chubby splotched frogs, and she told him that people in France ate the legs of frogs. They knelt by the pond and pretended to eat frogs' legs, passing each other an imaginary jar of pickled tamarind to liven up the slimy feast, until *Ma* called them in before the mosquitoes set upon them.

Debi told him about her little brother who lived in a state called Minnesota, and had never seen a mango or a tamarind pod. She told him how the snow piled up outside her house, and how on some days they couldn't go to school. Instead, they built tunnels and forts in the snow and fought battles with snow that they patted in their hands and made into little cannonballs. They had a bully in their neighborhood—like the big boys in the market here who sat at the soft-drinks stall all day—but he was rather slow. So they dared him to lick the railing near the railway tracks and his tongue got stuck to the metal because of the cold. Aleem had to ask his science teacher to explain the cleverness of this prank.

Aleem showed Debi a delicate fern, whose entire frond was smaller than his ten-year-old hand. Looking up at her expectantly, he touched it. As if a shiver had run down its spine, the frond closed. Debi drew a sharp breath. 'That's amazing. What is that?'

'A *lajjabati*. A shy girl.'

They checked the dictionary, but its knowledge did not stretch to obscure reaches of botany. They went to the school library, which was also proved incapable.

It was just a few weeks later that he came home from school and found *Ma* sitting on Debi's bed, folding her *shalwar kameez*. On Debi's desk was a tiffin box, packed with food that

was still hot, the lids unbuckled to let out the steam. Debi
was on a corner of the bed, wrapping her pair of everyday
sandals in a jute wrapper. Neither of them looked at Aleem.
Debi's backpack, which had been emptied and hoisted on
top of the clothes cupboard the day she arrived, lay open-
mouthed on the floor.

'Where are you going?'

'Go wash your hands and feet. I'll get some snacks for
you,' *Ma* intervened.

Debi did not look up. Aleem stood at the door until *Ma*
got up and steered him to the bathroom. When he came to
the dining table, she laid out his food silently and poured
him cold water. He asked if Debi was leaving, and *Ma* told
him she needed to see her family and they would have to say
goodbye to her. He loitered around her door later, but Debi
did not look up or even shift from her position. She held
the sandals in their jute wrapping on her lap and looked at
them. *Baba* came home and sent Aleem to his friend's house,
despite it being a school day. When Aleem came back for
dinner, Debi stayed in her room. *Ma* said, 'Poor, innocent
girl.' *Baba* did not answer.

The speeches are made and dinner is served. He is assigned
to another table, but after dessert and another speech when
everyone clinks their glasses together, she gets up and moves
from table to table. She touches someone's back and leans
in to laugh. After all the tables, she approaches the band of
waiters near the kitchen doors. One by one, they shake her
hand, and when she sees him she pauses, holding his hand.
'Where are you from?'

He tells her. She brings her eyebrows together for just a

moment, then a smile slowly rises to her lips. 'I know it a little bit. Which part are you from?'

He tells her. 'I'm much older now, but I am Aleem. I was only ten then. I'm at the university here now, doing a PhD. I just came last year. I didn't know you lived here. I'm sorry you had to see me.' He tried to stop after each thought but could not.

She still held his hand in hers. 'Little Aleem, little brother, *bhai*.'

'We didn't know where you had gone.'

She let out a long breath.

What happened to Debi? Why did she go without even talking to me? Did she not like our house? Were you too strict with her? For weeks, Aleem badgered his parents. She had to go back, they explained. They were more patient with him than he had ever known them to be. He heard them talk between themselves, with their relatives, talk about her honour. Her shame. But these were words that to him had no physical form, no literal meaning. He did not know to match them to the big boys with the untranslatable words in the market who had followed Debi around.

It was a few years before Aleem understood that their words had ripened into plans for an afternoon when Debi would be walking home alone through the market—the place creaking under the weight of jackfruit and red chilis and bright plastic houseware, and reeking of dried fish—past the old abandoned machinery depot with its rusting mid-century hardware, at the same time that the boys would be inside, high on *ganja*.

She asks about *Ma* and *Baba*, about the town, and about

how he got from school to college and now here. She asks him to visit her at her law offices and hands him her card. He shakes her hand as if she were someone he had just met, and watches her walk away.

Three days later, he puts on his only shirt with a collar, prompting his roommate to look questioningly at him. He catches the bus downtown, and looks alternately at the street signs and her card till he finds the low-rise corporate building. An assistant in very high heels shows him in, and she is sitting behind a dark grey desk with a matte metallic shine. She comes around and hugs him, and he says without intention, 'You look well, you look so well.'

She pulls back and holds him by his shoulders. 'I am well. It took me years, but I am well.'

She has never made her case public, and Volunteer Away is grateful. 'I didn't want to think about it or talk about it for the longest time.' Aleem turns away. He doesn't want to hear about it. He is ashamed, for those boys, for his town. She says it could have happened anywhere, to any young woman. She wants him to hear about meeting other rape survivors and how that helped her.

'When I was better, I didn't want to remember my assignment for only that.' She wants to remember it for Aleem, his parents, the school children, and the teachers. And the recycled-paper man.

Her parents think that the media may find a connection between her and Aleem and try to buy his story. But if she knows Aleem, her little brother, he would not contemplate such a thing.

He says seriously, 'I have no story. I didn't even know what had happened until I was older.'

Before he leaves, she says, 'I want to show you something. As soon as I had access to an encyclopedia, I looked it up.'

They go to her computer screen and she types in 'lajjabati'.

'Touch-me-not' shine the black letters on the glowing screen.

Bookends

Munize Manzur

From: Arbaaz Rahman <arbaazra.bd@gmail.com>
To: Zara Rahman <Zara.rahman@gmail.com>
Date: Thu, Sep 3, 2010 at 8:31 AM
Subject: An Enquiry
Mailed-by gmail.com

Dear Ms Zara Rahman,

My name is Arbaaz Rahman.

I am writing to you because I have been looking for a certain Zara Rahman for many years now. Twenty-three years, to be exact. I currently live in Dhaka, Bangladesh—a city with limited facilities for finding missing persons. In our society, we have what is called 'word of mouth'. It's a tight-knit place where news flies faster through the grapevine than the telegraph wire. But... I digress.

Ever since I lost my Zara Rahman, I have been looking for her everywhere. You must be thinking: what kind of person disappears into thin air? Ah, but that was the beauty of Zara. She could not be contained. So why am I looking for her two decades later? To ask her one simple question.

I have been holding on to this question—hoping that

if I ever bump into her, I shall finally be able to settle this irksome feeling. But I have never bumped into her.

I got married. I bought a house. I rose up the ladder. I made money. I hired people. I fired people. I ate. I slept. And I continued to dream of finding my Zara Rahman. Walking through crowds, my ears subconsciously scanned my surroundings for that familiar lilt of her voice, but did not register even a blip. At a restaurant once, my heart raced because I thought I caught a whiff of that familiar scent. But, no, I never bumped into her.

Recently, circumstances have led me to change my residence. I now live in a duplex apartment with my sister and her family. My nephew has installed a Wi-Fi (wireless something... I don't know what the 'fi' stands for...), which gives us 24-hour access to the Internet. I'm not sure if this is a curse or a boon. Some days I navigate through so many web pages that I lose track of where I started and where I wanted to go. My nephew teases me, saying that I am behaving like a child with a new toy. I should be embarrassed, except I have an informal relationship with him, so I simply laugh it off.

A few days ago he asked me, '*Mama*, what are you looking for?'

Absent-mindedly I replied, 'Zara Rahman.'

Next thing I knew, he bent down to the keyboard, typed in a few words, hit the enter key with a confident tap, and there, floating before my eyes, were 39,300 entries in 0.22 seconds. Amazing. To be searching for just one person for 23 years and then getting thousands of them in 0.22 seconds. This world can be scary with its instant gratification sometimes. Now my nephew has helped me narrow down the search. And I am left with about 8 possible Zara Rahmans.

You are one of them... Zara.rahman@gmail.com

Are you the Zara I am looking for? And if you are, will you untangle yourself from this giant web and meet your Arbaaz? Will you answer the one question I have been phrasing and rephrasing for the last two decades?

Sincerely,

Arbaaz Rahman

D.O.B.: 28 February 1959

S/O: Mr Abraar Rahman

Home town: Dhaka, Bangladesh

· ·◆◆◆◆· ·◆◆◆◆· ·

From: Zara Rahman <Zara.rahman@gmail.com>
To: Arbaaz Rahman <arbaazra.bd@gmail.com>
Date: Fri, Sep 4, 2010 at 10:01 AM
Subject: Re: An Enquiry
Mailed-by gmail.com

Dear Mr Arbaaz Rahman,

Thank you for your email. You must be either a lawyer or a doctor by profession. Your email made quite a compelling case without revealing anything of substance. And you wrote a lot of things as if by way of explanation, but it merely left the reader even more confused. Final diagnosis remained unknown.

One of the things I find most fascinating about this Internet business is that it allows you to be free of physical boundaries or politically drawn territories. You write that you are from Bangladesh, but really who can evaluate the truth except you? In fact, how is one to even know that you are truly who you claim to be? Mr Arbaaz Rahman, D.O.B.:

28 February 1959. S/O: Mr Abraar Rahman. How do I know this for sure?

It seems to me that if you are that keen to find this Zara Rahman, then you must convince her to step out from the line-up of 8. Which makes me wonder: is it possible that you have never bumped into her because *she* does not want to bump into you? And if that is so, why should she step out from behind her carefully woven curtain at your behest? The audience may clap as hard as they please, but sometimes an encore isn't possible because the time has run out. Anyway, what makes you so special to her? Perhaps, in the '23 exact years' you mention, she has made a life for herself in which she sees no role for you.

As for the irksome feeling, that is your itch to scratch. You should give up such phantom sensations and look for the real sore. The source of the infection. You have mentioned your life of eating, sleeping, and being merry. Why do you want to stir up what is obviously a nicely doctored life?

At 51, you are too old to be going on some wild goose chase. Or rather, some uncontained woman chase. Better, I think, to leave such energetic adventures to your young nephew. The one who can find 39,300 people in 0.22 seconds. You said you are married. For how many years? Anyway, stick to her, that chosen one. Don't let 0.22 seconds disturb all those years of marital harmony.

That is my advice to you.

Sincerely,

Zara Rahman

From: Arbaaz Rahman <arbaazra.bd@gmail.com>
To: Zara Rahman <Zara.rahman@gmail.com>
Date: Sat, Sep 5, 2010 at 7:54 AM
Subject: Re: An Enquiry
Mailed-by gmail.com

Dear Ms Zara Rahman,

I am sorry if my email has inconvenienced you in any manner. That was not my intention. I suppose you must not be the Zara I am looking for. My Zara wouldn't need to ask such suspicious questions. She always had an instinctive understanding of me.

We used to joke that she was the Z to my A. We were A to Z, a complete set by ourselves. The last letter 'z' in my name meant I was destined to be led to her, and the last letter 'a' in her name meant she was destined to be led to me, and we were looped in together. Even our last names were the same, so we felt that our forefathers had joined us cosmically way back when. Intertwined together on many levels to create a richer texture in each other's lives.

I met her at my friend Ratul's dinner party. She was 32 to my 28 years. It was a casual gathering of sorts. I almost didn't go because I had another dinner. But my friend was most insistent that I come, no matter how late. So when I turned up at around midnight, the party was in full swing. Lots of people scattered around the house. Talking, drinking, laughing.

The lights in the living room were turned down low and the furniture had been pushed aside to make a temporary dance floor. A heart-pumping rhythm pulsed out: "*Shout, shout, let it all out, these are the things I can do without, come on,*

I'm talking to you, come on!" What was that band called? I forget. But I remember the lines. Because that was the exact moment I saw her. Long curly hair, a flash of silver jewellery, blue jeans, some sort of off-the-shoulder t-shirt that clung in all the right places. She was dancing with Ratul, kohled eyes sparkling, fire engine-red lips fiery hot. My throat felt dry, so I swallowed. It hurt to swallow. I wasn't sure why.

She turned to the right, tapping out some rhythm in her head, and our eyes met. A slow blink, a curl of the lips, time measured in milliseconds. Then whoosh! She swung her head and the connection was lost in the indigo blackness of her hair. Ratul saw me and waved. When the song finished, he walked up, arm in arm with her.

'Arbaaz, you made it!' He gave me a friendly whack on the shoulder. I nodded, eyes darting to his companion.

Noticing this, Ratul said, 'Have you met Zara? She's visiting Dhaka for a while.'

Up close she was even lovelier. Creamy coffee skin, thick eyelashes.

'Nice to meet you,' I said.

'Is it?' she asked. 'How do you know?'

'Excuse me?'

'How do you know it's nice to meet me? You don't know me. How do you know I'm nice?'

That was the beginning of many questions. The three months that I got to know her, she was always full of questions. Probing and poking. Forcing me to see things askance. Turning my head with those deft fingers, making me think of answers to her questions.

Oh, but you don't want to know all these details. Perhaps I gave out more information than you needed. I'm taking a chance, hoping that if you knew some of these details, you would take pity on me and help me find Zara. So I can ask that last question, complete my set of answers and file it away once and for all.

You're absolutely right in that I should not disturb her life after all these years. I won't. She can choose to answer or ignore. I just need to ask.

I hope I was better able to make you understand my quest.

Sincerely,

Arbaaz Rahman

From: Zara Rahman <Zara.rahman@gmail.com>
To: Arbaaz Rahman <arbaazra.bd@gmail.com>
Date: Sat, Sep 5, 2010 at 1:43 PM
Subject: Re: An Enquiry
Mailed-by gmail.com

Dear Mr Arbaaz Rahman,

Please stop writing to me. I am not interested in your expired nattering. It doesn't matter what age you men are, you're all the same. You're never happy with what you have. You want what you cannot get. When you do get it, you don't know what to do with it. And so when you lose it, you go looking for it. Because you're never happy with what you have. Etc., etc., ad infinitum, ad nauseam.

You chose to answer my question about Zara. But you ignored the point I raised about the woman with whom you've been sharing your life all these years. Your wife. She made a life with you. Unlike your flighty Zara who left you in a mess of question marks and exclamation scars. Do you know what type of woman asks so many questions? The bipolar, manic sort. You're better off without her.

By the way, the band 'Tears for Fear' sang 'Shout, Shout'. You know, the universe works in mysterious ways. It gives us hints all the time, but too often we are ignorant of the clues. You should have known right away that any woman you see while listening to a shouting song sung by a highly emotional group (Tears? Fears??)is bad news. It even hurt for you to swallow. You should have run for the door while you still could.

Sincerely,

Zara Rahman

From: Arbaaz Rahman <arbaazra.bd@gmail.com>
To: Zara Rahman <Zara.rahman@gmail.com>
Date: Sun, Sep 6, 2010 at 6:42 AM
Subject: Re: An Enquiry
Mailed-by gmail.com

Dear Ms Zara Rahman,

No matter what I write, you are determined to demonise me. Why is that?

I chose not to mention my wife because there is no angst there. But you are right, humans spend more time on the agony than the ecstasy. Something that's true for men as well as women though, don't you think?

My wife and I got married about 20 years ago. I met her just once before I agreed to marry her. By then Zara had whirled a hurricane inside me and left me twirling without waiting for the dust to settle. I found myself wanting shelter, just some peace and quiet. Sufia with her dimpled smile, her kind eyes was exactly that. She loved me just as I was; she always made me feel like a good man. Whatever I did was good enough for Sufia.

The difference is… Zara made me want to become better than 'good enough'. I already had a good job in Standard Chartered Bank. My boss told me I had promise and if I put in the hours I could make it right to the top. Zara came into my meticulous office, juggled the paperweights on my table, scattered carefully filed papers, and unearthed gnawing worms lurking underneath. 'Is this what you want to be all your life? A banker? How mummifying!' Two questions, one statement… and the infinite hair on the back of my neck rose.

My first instinct was a defensive outrage. Who was she to judge me? Some editor working for a small-time publisher! Reading the words of strangers, but never finding the courage to show her own to anyone. Zara had told me she was working on her Great Bengali Novel. But she refused to show me her work. In fact, I doubted she had even written a page of it.

At least I was pursuing my dream and career simultaneously, I argued back. I showed her some of my photos. Photography had been a passion of mine from a very young age. But when you were the only son of a widowed mother, you learned very quickly that passion and profession did not necessarily meet. So I dabbled in it when I could. And pushed papers the rest of the time, like I should. Printing photos wasn't going to repay the mountain of debt my father had left us on when he suddenly died of a heart attack at 51. Photographing golden sunrises wasn't going to lead to my sister walking into the sunset with a graduate degree in hand. Someone had to be practical. And that someone had to be me.

To give her credit, Zara listened. Head tilted, as was her customary habit, chewing the inside of her cheek, she held my gaze until I was done. But the more I looked into those dark pools, the more I fell. Headfirst. Silently paddling, listening to the sound of my breathing, trying to find my rhythm. When I finally admitted that, yes, I missed photography, she smiled her sunshiny smile. Even today, when I see a rebellious ray of sunshine bursting through dark clouds, I remember that smile of hers.

'Fine,' she said. 'Let's do this. You dust off your cameras and start clicking within your soul again. And I'll finish my great novel.'

I don't know if she ever did. She left before I could find out. But whatever little I later saw of her work in progress was superb. I have been keeping an eye on new South Asian fiction all these years, but so far none of what I have come across bears her name. In fact, now that I think about it, if she had completed her novel, surely it would have shown up on that Web search?

Sorry if I troubled you. Desperate men take desperate measures. I just thought I would make one last ditch effort in my quest. Before it's too late.

Sincerely,

Arbaaz Rahman

From: Zara Rahman <Zara.rahman@gmail.com>
To: Arbaaz Rahman <arbaazra.bd@gmail.com>
Date: Sun, Sep 6, 2010 at 3:29 PM
Subject: Re: An Enquiry
Mailed-by gmail.com

'Before it's too late'… for what?

Don't tell me that you are dying and this is how you are spending your last moments on earth. Only a Bengali would come up with such melodrama!

What do you care whether she finished her novel? You got what you wanted. You managed to be the good son, faithful banker, dutiful husband, and recognised photographer in your own right.

Yes, I googled you. Impressive collection of awards. And I saw the photos you put up on Flickr.com. Some of them are better than others. You have a knack for composition. The album titled 'Bookends' is all of one woman. Is that your wife or Zara?

Strange title for a photo collection of a woman you seem quite enamoured of. The way your camera focuses on eyelashes dipped to meet the rising steam from a hot cup of tea. Hands cupped around a mug. Quite poetic, really. There's one of her sleeping curled on a beach chair. Where is that? Not sure the angle works there. She looks more like a blurb than one worthy of verse. Or is that what you were aiming for?

You've caught a wide range of expressions. She had about 29 different ones in an album of 40 photos. Veins popping out, neck curving away. A teasing smile. Glistening eyes.

Sitting petulantly on the sandy mound with sun setting (or was it rising?). Sprawled on the bed, face thrown back against the foot of the bed. I thought her candid ones were much better than the posed ones, though.

Anyway, I would have posted my comments on your web page, but since we had this thread of emails going, I decided to send the feedback here.

Best of luck to you.

Zara Rahman

⟡ ⟡

From: Arbaaz Rahman <arbaazra.bd@gmail.com>
To: Zara Rahman <Zara.rahman@gmail.com>
Date: Sun, Sep 6, 2010 at 10.28 PM
Subject: Re: An Enquiry
Mailed-by gmail.com

Ms Zara,

You said men don't know what they want. Sometimes, it seems, neither do women. You said not to write, and yet you do not snip off this 'thread'.

But I shall not look the proverbial gift horse in the mouth. I have long since mastered the art of being happy with what I have, for as long as I have it.

So thank you for your kind comments. The album 'Bookends' was my re-initiation into photography. Remember I told you how Zara had egged me into picking up my camera? I did. She and I went off to Cox's Bazaar (which is the longest unbroken sandy beach in the world, in case you didn't know) for a weekend. I toted my camera, she tucked in her pen and diary, we tossed some clothes and lots of music into a couple of duffel bags, and off we went. Very efficiently packed, as it turned out.

That weekend in Cox's was one of the most memorable in my life. We explored the land around us—stopping as we liked, surging forth as we wished. We explored the space between us—licking and flicking, engorging and engulfing. 'Steaming since morn. Moaning till dawn'—her lines, not mine. And we explored undiscovered shores to stake claims on. She with her writing.Me with my photography. We twisted and bended. Tao and Zen. Ducked and dove. Swooping, scooping, stooping to pick up perfected pebbles on the beach. I kept some of those. Occasionally I bring them out to see them, feel them, and wonder why we never got a chance to repeat such an experience.

Why did she leave without saying anything? She just packed her bags and went back to London. We didn't have an argument. We didn't have any misunderstandings. If anything, the weekend getaway was perfect and things kept getting better for us. True, we hadn't discussed a future together—but with such organic chemistry, it was a foregone conclusion. I never suspected that she harboured any doubts about that.

I remember one evening we made anagrams with our names, trying to see what other names could be made by combining our own. Zamara, Azaan, Zaraan, Arman, Arhaam. Neither of us said anything, but silently I felt as if we were listing our children's names. What kind of woman just ups and leaves in the middle of such quiet understanding? No war, yet one casualty.

Arbaaz

From: Zara Rahman <Zara.rahman@gmail.com>
To: Arbaaz Rahman <arbaazra.bd@gmail.com>
Date: Mon, Sep 7, 2010 at 9:51 AM
Subject: Re: An Enquiry
Mailed-by gmail.com

Perhaps a woman best forgotten. A woman who may have realised that when you live a lifetime in a moment, there can be no sustainable future. The perfect present tense does not easily translate into the future continuous tense.

Who knows??

Why are you so stuck in your past? You had a great time. It ended when it ended. You found someone else. Got married. You even had a list of baby names ready at hand. I don't see the dilemma here.

You met serendipitously. Seems fitting that you parted the same way. Otherwise God knows what black hole this twisted woman would have dragged you into.

By the way, you didn't answer why you chose that title for your album.

Zara

From: Arbaaz Rahman <arbaazra.bd@gmail.com>
To: Zara Rahman <Zara.rahman@gmail.com>
Date: Mon, Sep 7, 2010 at 12:10 PM
Subject: Re: An Enquiry
Mailed-by gmail.com

Black hole? No. We were pure light in a black hole. You have no idea how refreshing it felt to be unguarded with someone.

If you have ever lived in Dhaka, you will understand what I mean.

> For I have known them all already, known them all:—
> Have known the evenings, mornings, afternoons,
> I have measured out my life with coffee spoons;
> I know the voices dying with a dying fall
> Beneath the music from a farther room.
> So how should I presume?

Thus wrote T.S. Eliot in 1917. An uncanny prophet. One who foretold the predicament of a Bangladeshi man some 70 years later. This woman asked me things that I did not dare ask myself, and because of her I realised that all the answers I thought I had …were actually not mine. They had been superimposed on me as a son, a brother, a fitter-inner trying to cram myself into a box.

I didn't know what I wanted to do, but Zara helped me realise what I didn't want to do. Does that make sense? I didn't want a boring bank job. I wanted to travel. Rio in April. Paris in September. Trekking through India. Sitting atop a mountain in Bhutan. I'd never been to London. So maybe Zara and I could have gone off to London together if only she had waited for us to sort out the details.

But she never gave me that chance. Zara and I were meant to be bookends. Propping up a lifetime of words and poetry and experience between the two of us. Expanding, converging, circumscribing life as we pleased. Hence the album name. When she left…I lost my stand.

Yes, I moved on with my life. But I didn't take flight. Do you have any idea how hard it is to flutter your wings but not let loose? I got up early to catch the worms. I roosted. I nested over an empty feeling.

Which got transcribed into my marital life, too. Sufia and I never had children. We tried and tried. IVF, homeopathy, acupuncture. You name it, we did it. But to no avail. I think what was worse is the doctors couldn't tell us why. Each of us felt guilty. Then incomplete. Then resentful. Then depressed. Stone walls. Stonier silences. Sitting at the breakfast table, chewing our toast, trying to digest indigestible thoughts. We never argued. That would have denoted some emotion, whereas we had none to share. Our divorce a couple of years ago went through without a nick or a gash. Just two quick dashes of the pen.

I need to find Zara. To ask her: what did I do to make her leave me so cruelly? Why did she disappear on me?

From: Zara Rahman <Zara.rahman@gmail.com>
To: Arbaaz Rahman <arbaazra.bd@gmail.com>
Date: Mon, Sep 7, 2010 at 6:55 PM
Subject: Re: An Enquiry
Mailed-by gmail.com

You didn't do anything, Arbaaz. It was the thought of what you were *not* going to do that made me leave.

I remember every detail of our three months together. I remember our conversations, our laughter, our creations, our loopy loony talks. I had never met anyone like you. So serious, so sure of what he wanted out of life, so sure he would get what he wanted. You had your focus. I felt like I had been spinning in my head until I finally found you. How ironic that you felt freer when you met me. I felt like I had found my place when I met you.

But the thought that I was going to take you away from all that you needed to do—I couldn't bear it. You asked: 'What kind of woman just ups and leaves in the middle of such quiet understanding?' Simply put: a woman who quietly understood that she was standing between a man and his responsibilities.

How could I allow you to do something that you would possibly regret for the rest of your life? And then resent me for it… and then, us…

You're right in that we had a connection on many different levels. And part of that culminated in my understanding you better than you understood yourself at times. I never got over the… miracle… of that. That you certified me and all my craziness even before I recognised it. And that I knew you were too good a man to ever do injustice to another.

Do you remember October 17th? We couldn't get enough of each other that night. Conversing, silently communing. You with me and I with you, you in me and I in you. The conversation played on for hours. Long deep sweet plays. With the scratches and the jumps. The needle and the vinyl. Together there was music, and the times in between when we stopped to talk, there were lyrics. Then there came that moment when I had stars bursting all around me and I was left gasping, when every crevice of my body was filled by you and every pore oozed of you and you and you. I remember pulling your head towards me, wanting to anchor by your lovely dark-brown eyes while your body enfolded waves onto me . But do you know what I saw in your eyes? A stab of pain. A slight wince. The look a person gets when something new that he's been so enthusiastic about pinches him unexpectedly. You had the painful realisation that you would have to disappoint your mother and your sister in order to love me and live with me.

I was never going to live in Dhaka. I would have suffocated in that walled-in, pegged-down society long term. I had gone to visit for a few months. I never expected to fall in love. And you know me...I could never stay fallen for long. That was just not part of my psyche. If you were to stay with me, you would have had to fly away with me. Not just to another land. I would have insisted on sailing through risky uncharted waters. We both knew your mother wouldn't approve of me—older woman, unknown lineage, liberal arts education. If you had chosen me over all those better-suited Bengali women, you would have been forever flitting between a stony mother and a hardened wife.

You realised all this. And I realised that when you realised it, I couldn't do that to you. I couldn't make you choose between your rights versus your responsibilities. That was not the kind of woman I wanted to be.

So I made the choice. I left.

Zara

- ·»»» · ««·· ·

From: Arbaaz Rahman <arbaazra.bd@gmail.com>
To: Zara Rahman <Zara.rahman@gmail.com>
Date: Mon, Sep 8, 2010 at 8:25 AM
Subject: Re: An Enquiry
Mailed-by gmail.com

That was *not* your choice to make, Zara!

That was *not* your choice to make!

We were a set, a team, a pair of bookends. We were

opposing forces that combined and made sense, that had a purpose. You had no right to pull out on your own. You had no right!

You know what I think? I think that's your justification to yourself. You used me, my family situation, my reality, to avoid your real issue. You knew you could never ground yourself to anything or anyone permanently. You were a great one at anchoring by dark shores. But you could never stay aground. You feared long-term commitment. You knew that and so you made up this... this... pathetic reason.

I cannot believe I spent all these years berating myself. Wondering what I did wrong. When all this time it was you and your shortcomings that were responsible for what happened. So many wasted years I spent preserving your image! You turned out to be nothing but a mirage.

Arbaaz

From: Zara Rahman <Zara.rahman@gmail.com>
To: Arbaaz Rahman <arbaazra.bd@gmail.com>
Date: Mon, Sep 8, 2010 at 1:23 PM
Subject: Re: An Enquiry
Mailed-by gmail.com

Perhaps you're right. Perhaps I couldn't own up to my shortcomings, my issues of commitment and non-commitment, and took the easy way out in projecting them onto you. At any rate, I learned my lesson. God, with His great flair for irony, made sure of that...

What difference does it make anyway?

You led your life. You did all the things you should

have done. No one got hurt. You even made good as a photographer.

I never asked you to preserve my image. If I am a mirage, it's because you were thirsting for something. Perhaps you should ask yourself what that is.

Zee

· -⤜⤜⤜· ·⧯⧯⧯- ·

From: Arbaaz Rahman <arbaazra.bd@gmail.com>
To: Zara Rahman <Zara.rahman@gmail.com>
Date: Mon, Sep 8, 2010 at 8:03 PM
Subject: Re: An Enquiry
Mailed-by gmail.com

Zee...

I'm tired. I've been looking for you for too long to let it end like this. But I don't want to do this via email anymore. Can we meet?

I don't know where you live. These email addresses obviously do not carry any indication of the geographical locations. I've already told you I live in Dhaka. So is there a possibility for us to meet face to face?

Arb

· -⤜⤜⤜· ·⧯⧯⧯- ·

From: Zara Rahman <Zara.rahman@gmail.com>
To: Arbaaz Rahman <arbaazra.bd@gmail.com>
Date: Tue, Sep 9, 2010 at 1:15 AM
Subject: Re: An Enquiry

Arb,

I would certainly like to meet. For old time's sake. Not just because you were a love of mine. But also because you were one of the closest friends I ever had.

But my life is not mine alone to manoeuvre. I have a family to consider. The physical distance is not the issue here. Before we take steps towards each other, should we not consider the ramifications of what is at stake?

Are you ready to face up to what may happen after we meet? Are you sure you want to run the risk of offsetting your carefully balanced life, set up there in your duplex with your family and 24-hour Wi-Fi? Perhaps the virtual world is better, less complicated, than reality…?

Zee

From: Arbaaz Rahman <arbaazra.bd@gmail.com>
To: Zara Rahman <Zara.rahman@gmail.com>
Date: Tue, Sep 9, 2010 at 6:39 AM
Subject: Re: An Enquiry

There you go again with your questions, Zee. Some things about you will never change, I suppose. Which is okay. Even now, I balance you because many things in my life have changed.

> But though I have wept and fasted, wept and prayed,
> Though I have seen my head [grown slightly bald] brought in upon a platter,
> I am no prophet—and here's no great matter;
> I have seen the moment of my greatness flicker,
> And I have seen the eternal Footman hold my coat, and snicker,
> And in short, I was afraid.

....

No! I am not Prince Hamlet, nor was meant to be;
Am an attendant lord, one that will do
To swell a progress, start a scene or two,
Advise the prince; no doubt, an easy tool,
Deferential, glad to be of use,
Politic, cautious, and meticulous;
Full of high sentence, but a bit obtuse;
At times, indeed, almost ridiculous—
Almost, at times, the Fool.

I grow old… I grow old…
I shall wear the bottoms of my trousers rolled.

I think it is safe to say that, like Prufrock, I have ultimately failed in making my beloved understand me. The fact that you made such an arbitrary decision on your own tells me this.

So no, I will not 'dare to disturb your universe'. Like the Old Fool, I shall retreat into my dignified solitude. I shall put aside my past dreams of romance and eke out the existence of a passionless old man.

Please let us meet. You, your husband, your children, and I. Just to reconnect as old friends, if not bookends.

I would like that very much.

Arb

· 〉〉〉 · 〈〈〈 ·

From: Zara Rahman <Zara.rahman@gmail.com>
To: Arbaaz Rahman <arbaazra.bd@gmail.com>
Date: Tue, Sep 9, 2010 at 6:39 AM
Subject: Re: An Enquiry

My dear sweet obtuse Fool,

You certainly haven't changed. Ever ready to make safe assumptions. It is not a question of you disturbing my universe. 'Passionless old man'? Oh, what heroic melodrama! Last I checked, passionless old men didn't go around searching for their beloved for two decades.

You can wear your trousers rolled if you want. Nothing wrong with showing some flesh! I still wear my sleeveless blouses (not the off-shoulder T-shirt though because, at 55, I find that it doesn't always cling to 'all the right places'!)

Yes, let us meet then. To paraphrase your personal prophet T.S. Eliot: *'Let us meet then, you and I, Now that the evening has spread against the sky...'*

But it will be only you and I. No husband. I never married. And not child'ren'…one son. His name is Azaan. He's 23 years old.

Your Zee

Mehendi Dreams

Lori S. Khan

A mist of sadness descended over Kajalie as she gazed at the paisley swirls of *mehendi* on her sister's feet. She still couldn't believe that Ayesha was getting married. It seemed not so long ago that they had been children, sharing secrets and eating mangoes under the billowing cascades of bed-sheets that *Amma* had given them to act out their fairy-tale games.

She remembered how she and Ayesha would take *Amma*'s beaded and lace *dupattas*, wrapping the long scarves around themselves, and transforming instantly from ordinary girls into shy Bengali brides. It was strange, Kajalie thought, that the linen dreams and cotton hopes of two young girls had turned into a bejewelled reality for just one.

Tomorrow, Ayesha would be married, and everything would change. She would become a guest in their home from then on. There would no longer be any afternoons spent rolling on the floor in splits of laughter, only hushed giggles. New gossip would be introduced about people in Ayesha's life about whom Kajalie would know nothing.

Hiding underneath the dips and dots, twirls and swirls of dried *mehendi*, Kajalie was lost amongst the patterns; her thoughts lay scattered like the lines on the palms of her hand.

She tried to pretend that the crescent-shaped tears that were pooling in her eyes were for her sister, and not herself.

Kajalie had received three proposals, to Ayesha's twelve. It was understandable, given the fairness-obsessed society they lived in. Kajalie had been hearing it all her life: 'What did the bride look like? Was she *phorsha*? Hmm, too bad, she has a pretty face. I hope their children get the father's complexion.'

Kajalie knew that this was something Ayesha had never had to worry about, with her skin the colour of milk kissed by a hint of rose-petal pink. But it was something that Kajalie had been aware of—had been made aware of—all her life. Her caramel skin was no match for cream. Yes, it seemed that the whole of Bangladesh had forgotten that caramel was so much tastier than bland milk flavoured with rose petals!

And if caramel skin wasn't bad enough, she had recently become the extended family's favourite object of pity. 'Don't worry just because your younger sister is getting married before you. I am sure you will find someone.' '*Beta*, God has a plan for everyone. It's just not your time yet.'

Kajalie no longer wanted to hear from people about the role of destiny in one's life, about having to wait patiently for a supposedly right time that seemed to be forever in coming, and about the promise of a spouse out there for everyone. There were people who were getting married for the second time, and she still couldn't manage to find a first husband. What if these people had taken the partner that was supposed to be hers, she thought in sudden terror, as she wiped away the tell-tale trail of her tears.

And yet somehow, along with those tears, Kajalie gradually also began brushing away the feelings of sadness, humiliation, and emptiness. She shed them one shrivelled *mehendi* flake at a time. She wanted to believe that if she flicked at them long enough, maybe beneath the dried-up flakes of green and brown, somewhere the beauty of caramel tinged with red would begin to emerge.

Table for Three

Shazia Omar

I roll across our bed into the space where Asif has so recently been. The warmth energises me for the day. All is going well till I find a cockroach lurking by the sink. I launch my sandal at it, but miss, so I bathe quickly in fear of its reemergence. Asif is a sure shot when it comes to killing cockroaches. I wish he hadn't left so early.

The sky is waking from sweet dreams but I can't pause to enjoy the colours. My mother-in-law will be up soon, so I am in a rush to prepare breakfast. I prefer to cook in solitude.

Today she's up unexpectedly early, washing the dishes clean.

I fry three eggs—one for her, one for myself, and one for Asif. I lay ours on the table and pack his away for later. He's left for work, but will be hungry when he returns.

'What's that for?' she asks. I explain that it's for Asif, and she grimaces. Her eyes are blazing cannons. Nothing I do pleases her. I've been married to her son for twelve years and she still detests me.

She joins me at the table after washing her hands. She washes incessantly. She is petrified of germs. No amount of scrubbing can wash out the cesspool trenches in her heart. A blitz of brutal thoughts sweeps through my mind; I imagine tearing at her frail flesh with machetes. I loathe myself, am aghast at my intolerance; still, the silent tirade continues.

Ashamed, I try to focus on my plate. My egg is spicy, sprinkled with chili peppers. Hers is plain. We both like our eggs shot through with tomatoes, red and runny, like bleeding wounds. Asif doesn't like tomatoes. He prefers his eggs with coriander.

I attempt a truce by sparking up a conversation. I tell *Amma* that Asif is taking me out for dinner to celebrate *Pahela Baishakh*. She gives me a look that I hope is not jealousy, but I'm not sure. 'I'll make some chicken roast for you, so you won't have to worry,' I assure her.

She shakes her head, tired of my intrusions into her life. I want to remind her that it was she who chose me to marry her son, but I refrain. There's nothing to be gained from needless confrontations. '*Amma*, would you like a *paratha*?' I ask dutifully.

She mumbles under her breath. Sullen and cold, she leaves the table to open the windows and welcome the morning. I don't offer to help. I've learnt to avoid such landmines in the course of our interactions. Certain chores are her territory: the plants, the fridge, the dishes. She likes it that way. She feels I am not thorough enough.

Amma is nothing like her son. Asif is patient, accepting, encouraging. *Amma* is a vulture swooping over a blood-soaked battlefield. It makes me sad. I don't have a mother of my own. Asif says she loves me, even though she has a different way of expressing it.

After breakfast, I iron a red sari for myself and a maroon *kurta* for Asif. It's the one he wore on our first *Pahela Baishakh* together. I hope he'll take me out for Chinese, but he said it's a surprise, so I'm not sure what to expect.

The day drags on. The clock is frozen, leaving me trapped in a portal of timelessness. I dust and sweep as I wait for Asif. I watch *Amma* wash the dishes over and over again. I concentrate on chores to kill time. I wash the clothes and take them to the rooftop to dry. A flock of white birds flies towards me and then beyond. In V-formation. V for victory. The sight fills me with a fleeting sense of tranquility, I cannot explain why. I run out of clothes pins, so I return to our flat with a few items still soaking in the bucket. I need to go to the market to purchase some clothes pins.

I prepare *koi* fish with oranges for lunch. I can hear *Amma* in the bath. She bathes for three hours. She has a condition: obsessive compulsive disorder. Asif explained it to me. He says our children may inherit it, when we have children, because it's genetic. His *nani* had it too.

After her bath, I sit with *Amma* for lunch. She turns on the television. Soap operas on Channel Zee are the joy of her life. I am grateful for the break in monotony. We watch two shows, then retreat to our respective rooms.

Late in the afternoon, *Amma* complains about a smell. Together we search for the source and she discovers the bucket of laundry I had left by the door. I try to explain that I have to buy clothes pins, but she is furious, and I'm humiliated. She takes the clothes to the bathroom for a rewash and then tells me she will go up to the rooftop, to drape them over the clothes line, without pins. She says they won't blow away, not to worry, and I feel a little better; at least she's not angry anymore.

She returns from the roof unexpectedly soon, flustered.

'It's cloudy,' she says. 'Why did you wash the clothes?' Her voice is icy with reproof.

Tears sting my eyes. I can't explain it, I thought it was sunny. I didn't notice the clouds. 'Shall I collect the clothes?' I offer. She doesn't reply. I go with her to the rooftop. We collect the laundry and return to the apartment. We spread the clothes out on the furniture and turn the fans on high. The flat looks festive with the laundry laid out. I wonder if this is not a better method for us, but I keep the thought to myself.

In the evening, I browse through my wedding album. Asif looked handsome in his *sherwani*. I looked like a child, though I was already twenty. My eyes look frightened, though I remember being excited, not scared. Perhaps it was the makeup, applied with a heavy hand by the girls at the parlour. The album ends with photos from our honeymoon in Cox's Bazaar. We danced in the sand and swam in the waves. Asif took some lovely photos of me. I looked like a Channel Zee actress.

I'm feeling impatient. I try calling Asif, but his phone is busy. I shouldn't disturb him, but it's *Pahela Baishakh*. Even last night he came home late. Things are busy at work, he explained.

I decide to get ready before he gets home. I retrieve the expensive perfume from the *almirah* and spray my wrists. I put on my gold bangles.

The doorbell rings and I rush out of my bedroom, past *Amma*. I'm disappointed to receive mail from the guard. Why is he delivering it so late? Amma is staring at me with unambiguous disapproval. I return to my room and lie down. At some point, I surrender to sleep.

My daughter-in-law is a nut. I can't escape that reality. She is a certified lunatic.

I woke up early today because I was feeling sick. She was up too, before dawn. I wonder if she ever sleeps. I caught her ferreting away some eggs. She never ceases to amaze me.

She made us breakfast. She's a good cook—that I'll admit, though she's unclean. It's not that she chooses to be dirty. She's just absent-minded. I have to wash everything myself. I'm particular about cleanliness. I have a sensitive stomach.

I watered the plants today. They are in full bloom, flowers of a hundred colours. I thank them for growing so brightly for me. Asif said plants are life-affirming and they need love—not just water and sunshine—to grow. I cherish these plants; he gave them to me. Because of them, I make it to the verandah and end up getting some fresh air.

I say fresh, though the fumes in this city make it more like a gas chamber. Our flat feels like a prison sometimes, especially now that we never leave. Asif used to take us to the park in the evenings, but that was years ago.

My daughter-in-law cooked *koi* today, Asif's favourite fish. After lunch, she and I watched TV, the usual soap operas. The programmes these days are so different from the ones we used to watch on BTV when Asif was young—the Dynasty and MASH episodes that aired once a week. We would wait for them in anxious anticipation. Asif was crazy about MASH. That's where he first got the idea of joining the army. I should have discouraged him from the start, but I thought it was the kind of dream all little boys dwell in, one he would outgrow.

His grades were good. He stood First Class First in his HSC exams. He could have been anything he wanted: a doctor, or a lawyer perhaps. But of all things, he wanted to join the army! I blame my husband. His family had a number of military men. His own older brother—Asif's *Chacha*—was one, in fact. They must have somehow influenced him, no doubt about it.

Asif was tall and well-built, with 20/20 vision, so the Bangladesh army was happy to accept him. He quickly proved his worth, excelling in military boot camp, rising swiftly through the ranks. He was a deadly marksman. He never missed a shot, they said. Not that it helped much, when the time came.

After he turned twenty-five, I thought that if I found him a nice wife, she could help me convince him to pursue a different career; if nothing else, to join the detective branch or an intelligence agency. I guess she tried. She was as afraid of him going to fight as I was. But secretly she admired his courage, and I think that's what fuelled his determination to continue.

Courage? It's silly to call it courage. Or patriotism. Or anything golden. It is sheer foolishness to fight like barbarians over someone else's land or politics or beliefs. Such things need to be resolved through dialogue, and not by outsiders, either.

I never managed to convince Asif of that.

My daughter-in-law dressed up in a red sari today and waited for Asif to return 'from work'. I ate dinner alone, bitter. Unable to escape the gallons of perfume she had poured on herself, unable to tell her, yet again, that Asif is dead.

He died far away from us, in the dark heart of the Congo.

No matter how hard she tries to imagine it otherwise, she cannot bring him back.

But I suppose she's better off living in her fantasy—a place where the sun shines every day, and she waits for her doting husband to come home to her.

Gandaria

IFFAT NAWAZ

We lived in a big, ugly house when I was young. At least, that's what Ma always said. She said it had no form; it just grew without any advance planning, and with it grew the ugliness. When she got up every morning to make me breakfast before I went off to school, she would mutter under her breath, 'Yet another morning in this hellhole. What a pathetic pile of crap we live in!'

It *was* quite ugly, in fact. The house was in Old Town, in Dhaka. In Gandaria, to be precise. I hated that name. Gandaria—it sounded extremely unsophisticated to me. It was only recently that I found out that the name Gandaria is actually derived from 'Grand Area'. The name was shortened over time, and lost all its grandness in the process. Anyway, the point is I hated uttering the word Gandaria. When the girls at school asked, I would say I lived in Wari, which sounded way better and was supposed to be a bit more posh than Gandaria, though it was still in Old Town.

My grandfather had exchanged two houses with Hindus fleeing to India during the 1947 India-Pakistan partition; one was, in fact, in Wari, and the other in Gandaria. My family lived in the Wari house until I was born, and then for some godforsaken reason decided to move even further away from the centre of the city into the chaos of sweetshops and blind believers.

My grandfather, *Dada*, decided also to add a few new sections to the house. And being someone who believed in instant gratification, he simply hired construction workers and started building wherever he pleased. A new veranda in the middle of the house that was slightly tilted; a new room next to the kitchen which received no light and always smelt of day-old curry; and stairs in the middle of the dining room that led up to a bathroom. Yes, nothing really made sense in our big, ugly house in Gandaria.

But we still continued living there. My brother was born and brought back to that house. My parents left it for a year at a time on two occasions to finish their higher education degrees in the US. I broke my first set of teeth and grew them back. I even had my first crush, standing on the roof of that big, ugly house.

He was a shoemaker's son, untouchable.

He had mocha skin, big eyes, slanted in the corners, deer-like, full lips that carried the perfect amount of intelligence and allure. But then we spoke—and everything went wrong. His voice didn't go with that face, and his words didn't go with his physique. He left me with my very first disappointment as far as the male sex was concerned. I was about eleven at the time.

It was around then that Kushum came to stay with us, replacing another young maid who had left the previous month. She was a few years older than me—fair and short, with a thin wooden stick in her left nostril, where a nose ring was supposed to be. She had a round flat face with light brown eyes, and long hair that helped conceal her thinness.

The first thing my grandmother did to Kushum was shave all her hair off. According to, *Dadi*, she had lice. Kushum sat in our tilted verandah, shedding useless tears as her hair fell off her head like a series of dust bunnies. She looked terrible bald, but we got used to it in a day or two. And in a week, she knew not to sit on the sofas or eat from the same plates as we did. It was all part of the usual training of domestics that went on in most Bangladeshi households.

Before we knew it, months had gone by, and Kushum's hair grew back into a cute bob. She roamed around in my old dresses, with unmatched pajama bottoms, taking orders from members of the household and watching television during her little breaks.

The greatest number of orders came from my *Dada*. He was one of those men who went through several complicated steps in order to accomplish just one simple task. For example, he had separate *lungi*s to accompany each of his activities during the course of the day. One for *namaz*, one for relaxing and watching television while chewing *paan*, one for going out for his walks, and one for using the bathroom. Every hour he changed from one *lungi* to another, and screamed at the top of his lungs for things to be brought to him: his walking stick, or cubed papaya to snack on, or his spittoon, or a special *paan* made by my *Dadi*. The orders never stopped. Indeed, they grew with his age, and Kushum, being the good little worker that she was, fulfilled every single one of them with a smile.

My *Dadi* was quite pleased that her husband was so well taken care of, though she never expressed any gratitude towards Kushum. *Dadi* had separated her bed—in fact, her room—from my *Dada's* after my brother was born. No one thought anything of it, since it was because of me that *Dadi* had initially left *Dada's* bed. I had just started sleeping in my own room. Inevitably, I needed someone to sleep with me, because I was scared of the dark and the noises that only an old house in Old Town can make.

Besides, my *Dada* and *Dadi* hadn't had a great relationship for as long as I could remember. Their day started with both expressing their annoyance with each other, and continued with random outbursts of anger and shouting. At the end of it, still muttering something not so pleasant about *Dada*, *Dadi* would cut fresh fruit to be sent to her husband via Kushum. It was as if her anger were sprinkled like salt and pepper all over the grapefruit or pineapple, which my Dada gobbled up in just a few mouthfuls, oblivious to the bitterness with which the fruit was garnished.

So everyone found it strange when my *Dada* and *Dadi* sat together—right next to each other—for three straight days, talking in low voices, with no shouting or arguments. When I entered the room where they sat, I discovered them in intense conversation, their eyes locked into each other's gaze. There was something so fiery about the sight that I had to look away and blush. It was as if two old people were falling in love again, or if not in love, then in understanding at least.

During those three days, when *Dadi* came to bed, she didn't speak at all. Usually, she had a hundred things to say about the thousand things that I was doing wrong. It could be the mosquito net not tucked in right, or the bottoms of my feet being dirtier than usual. But during those days, there was not a peep from her. So instead I tried to make conversation. But she wouldn't respond, she would fall asleep almost instantly.

On the fourth day, there were tears. The intense meetings were over. *Dada* continued changing his *lungis* a few times a day, and ordering Kushum to fetch warm bath water and oil to be rubbed on his back. But my *Dadi,* she was still. She sat on the verandah and didn't move at all. From afar, she seemed to have a blank expression. But when we went closer, very close, we would find a tear or two resting in the corner of her eye.

Finally, Ma stepped in. She took *Dadi* to her room, and shut the door. The door remained shut the whole afternoon, and the mystery got thicker. When they came out of the room, Ma, too, looked as if she had been crying. When I asked her what the story was, she gave me a swift slap on my face and walked away. I stood there humiliated and dumbfounded, but then—like any normal twelve-year-old—got over it and went back to my chores.

All this while, the only person who had been continuing to live life without much of a reaction was Kushum. Her body was much plumper now. Her breasts were way fuller than those of most fourteen-year-olds. She had hips, too, and curves. Had she put on a sari, she would have looked like one of those newlywed wives who lets go right after the wedding and puts on a good few happy pounds. She bore a little smirk on her face all day long, as if she had been let in on some secret that the rest of us were not privy to.

There were many more meetings—Ma with Baba, Baba and Ma with *Dadi*. My aunts came, and they, too, had long meetings together. Then Baba and the aunts sat with *Dada* one day, which ended up in an orgy of tears. I was lost, really lost.

The only thing I noticed was that Kushum no longer took any orders from my *Dada*. She was forbidden to go to his room, and his door was always shut. Our fifty-five-year-old cook would bring food straight to my *Dada's* room, and a young boy was employed to take my *Dada's* orders. It felt like there were more changes to come, but I just couldn't figure out what they could be.

It was unbearable for me, not to be a part of all this. So one afternoon, when Kushum was lying on the floor of my room with her fuller-than-full body and her mysterious smirk, I asked her if she knew anything. She started laughing at my question, which got me really furious. Even the maid knew what was going on! I asked her to stop laughing and tell me right away what she knew. She didn't laugh this time, she bit her lower lip.

She was lying on her stomach. She lifted her head towards me and I could see her overdeveloped breasts bursting out of the old *kameez* of mine that she was wearing. She slowly sat up, seducing the air around her and whispered, 'You will understand when you grow up.' Then she got up and walked away, swinging her hips, looking back to wink at me.

My whole body felt a strange jittery, shivering sensation. It wasn't like a fever, rather a hot burst of energy that feels shameful and infectious—and, at the same time, addictive. She looked back at me again, and burst into loud laughter. And exactly at that moment, our big, ugly house in Old Town became even uglier, as blood poured out from between my legs and I grew up.

Rida

Rubaiyat Khan

Week 12

When I turned twelve and started to bleed, my mother began searching through the trashcan in the bathroom. She soon found the thick mesh of bloody discarded cotton that I had carried between my legs to stop the flow. I watched her in silence from behind the creased bathroom door. My mother unwrapped the old newspaper it was packed in, unfolded the cotton, and examined the blood before tossing it back in the can. At the time, I was repulsed—too afraid to bring it up, to ask her why she did it. When I turned fourteen, I understood. My mother didn't trust me. It was my age, she said years later, that made her do it. She did not distrust me, she said; she distrusted the foolish flights of fancy that seized young pubescent girls.

When I was twelve, my chest and limbs began to hurt. My breasts felt ripe, and assumed a conical shape that made me uncomfortable when I looked at them. I had started to develop earlier than the other girls in my class. I was no longer allowed to wear my blue skirt to school. Instead, I wore a long blue knee-length tunic with a white cotton scarf that hid my chest. When I went out to a friend's home, or a relative's place, my mother came into my room while I undressed, and wrapped a length of cloth tightly around my naked chest to flatten it. Sometimes, I found it difficult to breathe, but it never occurred to me to protest. I still look at my breasts in the mirror and blame my mother for the way they sag prematurely.

Week 20

Ma told the most beautiful tales while she oiled and braided my hair. She told me of how, when she was a young girl visiting her ancestral village, she had encountered a djinn. She was sitting on a low branch of her favourite guava tree one afternoon, and eating a ripe guava, when a little girl in a yellow frock came up to her and asked for a bite. She said the little girl's feet were twisted, distorted, and had assumed a bulbous shape, and she stood with the balls of her feet faced forward where her toes should have been. My mother, frightened at such a sight, had run away.

She told me how she would swim with the *koi* fish in her grandfather's pond. I imagined her as a young girl in a thin cotton tunic, plunging into moss-green, murky waters. In my mind's eye, she was nothing like she is now. She had a narrow waist, and long thick jet-black hair that reached down to her hips. Her skin was creamy yellow and smooth to the touch. She has shorn off her hair now, because the stagnating heat overwhelms her. She does not care because she wears the *hijab*, and no longer feels the need to display her beauty. She is barely able to walk because of the burden of her obesity. She suffers from Plantar fasciitis.

The lilt in her voice when my mother told me these stories, their musical quality, almost soothed me to sleep, until she tightened the braided knots into circular patches on my head and tied them in place with silk ribbons, finishing up the task.

I loved those blue silk ribbons, and I went to school wearing them. I could tell the other girls snickered behind my back. I hid at the back of my school during lunch breaks, and after school, I sought refuge in the dusty kindergarten playground where I didn't have to mingle with the others. I heard their chatter and laughter on the games field. They threw water on each other from their drinking flasks, and their shirts were covered in muddy dirt and grime. I turned my nose up at them, at their childishness. I told myself I didn't care that the girls hated me, and the boys made fun of me. I ignored the snide remarks and open scorn. Once a girl told me I was 'stiff', but I knew it was because she was jealous. I told myself that the girls envied my grace, and the dignity with which I carried myself. My silence was my biggest weapon. Maybe it still is.

Week 22

My mother bought the monthly groceries from the outdoor street bazaar in Mirpur, a place that still conjures up in my mind images of uneven streets covered in filth, blackened mud, faeces of stray dogs, spit and urine and human waste, and garbage spilling out of the rectangular open concrete enclosures meant to contain it, and the pervasive stinging ammoniac smell that assaulted your nostrils as you passed through. My mother went through that filth in a rickshaw, just to pinch a few more pennies than she would have been able to had she gone to a regular grocery store. She bought sacks of ground wheat that she made into perfectly round, flat chapattis in the kitchen, and served for breakfast. In the years to come, she reminded us of how she went out of her way to buy unadulterated wheat for the sake of our health, even if it meant that she had to carry two back-breakingly heavy sack loads at a time on the rickshaw, sitting with her legs hoisted on top of them during the journey home. That image remains embedded in my mind.

Whenever my mother went out to run an errand, I kept a vigil on the upstairs verandah. I watched the front gate like a hawk, always afraid that she wouldn't return, that she would die, and I would be left alone in the world. There was a disconnect from my father, who seemed to me austere, and inaccessible, and from my older brother, Mahmud, who lingered in solitary confinement in his own room, listening to music, his room clouded with cheap cigarette smoke. I stayed in my own room and wrote in my journal, and dreamt of my soulmate. I imagined this boy in school, the memory of whom I still love deeply, embracing me in a bubble that shielded us from the outside world—from the boredom of the dimly lit dining room where Mahmud and I hunched silently over our respective homework after evening prayers.

Week 24

I hadn't seen my mother in three years. It was the longest time that we had ever been apart. The last time I spoke to her was on the day of my departure with my new in-laws and husband, whom I had met five times before agreeing to be his wife. He was a good-looking man with deep-set eyes and an angular jaw, and in the picture that he sent my family during the initial phases of our arranged marriage, I had noticed his hands above all else. They were the hands of a man—large, yet somehow capable of tenderness, with a matting of hair that peeked through the cuffs of his blue shirt. Later, he would hold me up against the towel rack with those very same hands, and let me fall against the metal railing, sending me crashing to the floor. His beautiful hands would be splayed hard against my chest, so hard that I would feel as if my breasts were on fire. When I met him, he seemed to me to be the man I had been waiting for my whole life.

At the airport, my mother and I stood close to each other, grazing each other's bodies. I drew comfort from the feel of the familiar silk headscarf she always wore on special occasions. It held the faint vapour of her perfume, mingled with her sweat. I clasped her hand, and my fingers trembled.

Moments seared into my consciousness: I lie still in a room in a small two-bedroom apartment in Nairobi, Kenya, hardly breathing, as my mother-in-law screams outside at the black manservant. I can hear her voice piercing the thin wooden slab of a door. Every day it pervades my senses. Every day I wake up hearing her voice, and my feet and hands grow cold in bed.

I am not allowed to go out by myself. I am not allowed to write to my parents, to visit my aunt who is posted in Zimbabwe. The only thing I have in my possession is a notepad. I use it to record my life, to keep me sane. I try to make sense of my life, of my past, tracing out my life as if it were a map, trying to uncover its hidden purpose. I hide it deep in my closet, so that he can't find it.

He doesn't let me sleep at night. When he leaves for work with his father at dawn, I see them off from the balcony, still in my maroon cotton kaftan. I think of flying as I watch them leave. I think of crashing on the hard concrete floor several stories beneath me, next to the rows of fragile tulips and irises.

Moments seared into my consciousness: the maroon cotton kaftan, torn from side to side, bunched into the trashcan in my bathroom. I wonder what the black servant will think when he finds it there.

Week 26

Sometimes, when he was in a good mood, he took me out. We drove through winding streets and slopes, through village fairs and open markets. Gigantic birds perched atop trees that appeared storm-flattened. Kenya is a beautiful place. I especially loved the flowers that bloomed all over the countryside in a riot of colours. The thick, moist sweetness of their smell smothered your senses.

Once we drove through the Uhuru Valley. Uhuru, which means 'freedom' in the Kiswahili language, lies on the northern slopes of Mt. Kenya, near the town of Timau. We walked through the colorful Uhuru rose farm, and as we did so, I took his hand in mine, then leaned my head against his chest, taking in the damp smell of his sweat-stained shirt. He could be surprisingly tender, his voice like silk. He is your father.

Week 32

In my head, I am still there. I can't get out.

It was perhaps a premonition. In Bengali folklore, spotting an owl is a sign of bad luck soon to follow. An owl lingered in the backyard slopes one late evening, a few weeks before

I left him for good. I sat there with him, while he inhaled smoke deep into his lungs. He spoke tortuously, saying he had started drinking again only because of me, because he loved me.

The owl was floating like a silken sash in the air, gliding from one tree to another. Glow worms quivered and gleamed in the dark, as I felt his chest rise and fall next to me. He dragged on one cigarette after another, not entirely finishing the first, flicking it outwards from the balcony, the embers of the stub pulsating for a second before being consumed entirely by the darkness below. I didn't know you would take root inside me that night. He cried, and I felt his hot, damp tears against my neck. I held him in my arms, cradled him as though he were my child.

Week 36

You will be fully formed now, nestling inside me during my third trimester. You will weigh down my body. It is no longer only mine. It is your home. These days, we go shopping, my mother and I. I have been back for a while, living with her and my father. They have both grown so old. The bags under my mother's eyes and the stretch marks on her once flawless skin startle me. Mahmud has moved to the United States. He left soon after my whirlwind wedding. He writes me long letters now, says he loves me and would do anything to see me happy. I can tell he is lonely too.

When my mother and I go shopping, we move swiftly through aisles full of clothes or plastic Tupperware, not really looking at the merchandise. She selects an item of clothing and holds it against me; she asks me to put it on in the fitting room. I humour her and do so. When I come out, she exclaims, 'The colour is so beautiful. It suits you so well!' She happily tries on shoes, and momentarily forgets.

Once during one of our shopping expeditions, this time with my mother's best friend in tow, I see rows of shiny plastic baby bottles lining a shelf, and I think of you. As I finger them, I can sense her behind me, silently crying as she leans her head on her best friend's shoulder.

My daughter lies in her cot day and night in her orange cotton nightie and refuses to come out of her room. I am scared to knock on her door, but I make myself do it. Sometimes she gets angry, at other times she invites me in, allowing me to lie down next to her and watch television with her, pillows propped behind our heads as we stare at the bright screen.

I feed her dinner sometimes with my hand, when I get some respite from my work. I mash boiled rice and potatoes, together with lentils, just the way she likes it, and she lets me feed her. I shape the doughy rice into tiny balls. I try not to make them too large, for she has always complained that I make them too big and her cheeks stretch painfully because they can't contain the food. After the abortion, she hasn't been able to eat anything apart from this, developing an aversion to wonton soup in particular, because that is what she was fed after she came home from the hospital. The doctor told her to have only fluids afterwards, so I asked her father to get some soup from the nearby Chinese restaurant.

When she was wheeled back into the dim room where I waited for her after the operation, she was in a light blue gown, and she was so dizzy she couldn't keep her eyes open.

I helped her sit up on the bed, and her naked back peeked through the loosely tied straps of her gown. She hadn't been eating properly for some time, and her spine stood up in blocks on her neck.

When I looked at her sitting so helplessly on that bed, her bare legs dangling, I wanted to run a knife through my own heart, but instead I helped her put on the cotton pyjamas in which she had arrived. As she slipped into them, blood trickled down her thighs. My heart skipped several beats, and I prayed fervently, at that moment, for her not to notice this, for she was still dazed from the anaesthetic. Instinctively, I opened my mouth to speak, to react to whatever she would do next were she to notice. But she did nothing, only slipped the pyjamas on and tied the knot around her waist.

On my prayer mat, I sit night and day and say prayers for her, every kind of prayer that exists. I call out to God, the Merciful, the Beneficent. Sometimes I lose control, and weep so loudly I'm afraid she or my husband will hear me. Although I'm a strong woman, I cannot contain myself during prayer when I face Him, my Allah, because it was I who told my child with a hardened heart that I would not let her bring a baby into this world, and ruin her future forever. It was I who sharply reprimanded her, shook her by her shoulders till she sobbed, screamed at her, and told her she would have to listen to me.

I cry to God for forgiveness every day, continuously, when I see the soul no longer there in my daughter, when I see her walk around in the verandah aimlessly, lifelessly. But I stop the weakness of my tears before they overwhelm me. I have to breathe.

I have to go on, for my daughter.

Daydreams

SADAF SAAZ SIDDIQI

She usually woke up at dawn, the time of the *Fajr* prayers; an otherworldly window before reality intruded. Colours softer than sunset spread over the vast expanse, making her feel insignificant. The dust caught in her throat, disturbed up from the *jharu*, the broomstick made of dried grass twigs. One of her daily chores was sweeping the mud-paved courtyard surrounded by a cluster of hut-like houses, fortified with wavy tin and concrete. She liked to take her time, piling up the leaves. Later she would go to school, balancing on the narrow embankment that separated the rice-rich spaces.

Built in the typical government style of individual classrooms with verandas running the length of the building, the school would have been well ventilated had the electricity ever worked. Shewli was invariably just in time to take her place on one of the rickety benches at the back. She did love her school though, encountering new things and reading about far off places. Shewli had seen her mother doing the backbreaking work of planting the paddy and drying the rice, always the last to eat. She certainly didn't want to end up like that.

She listened eagerly to reports about visits to Dhaka

shohor, and watched with fascination the *tok shows* on the
TV in a nearby aunt's house. The women always appeared
so confident. She could spend hours secretly looking in her
small mirror, pretending to be like them. Her late father
would have called her *behaiya*, a woman with no morals,
had she thought of going anywhere without a *dupatta*
covering her head. He had passed away after a road accident.
Her paternal uncles sent her mother, her siblings and herself
back to live with her maternal uncle, after her father died.
Her *Mama* had agreed to take his sister in, despite protests
from his wife, Nasima *Mami*. Hence they were now living in
a hut at the back of their compound. She had to be on her
best behaviour, her mother explained to Shewli.

She dreaded the day when she might have to stop going
to school. 'She will get married; there's no point in feeding,
clothing and educating a girl,' her mother had to constantly
hear from relatives. Shewli felt a wave of resentment when
reminded of her limitations as a girl. She was better than
the scraggy village boys, whether it was climbing trees or
coming first in school, despite their roaming freedom. She
silently rebelled at the increasing restrictions imposed on her
due to her coming of age and her 'orphaned' status. She had
tacitly promised her mother that she wouldn't be 'insolent'
at her *Mama's* place, which essentially meant she couldn't
question anything.

Shewli had thought of getting a job, as her cousin
Salma had, in Dhaka. Apparently garments factories were
employing women even if they hadn't worked before. Salma
shared a room with other girls, and even earned enough to
pay for her brother's private tutor. Shewli thought of them
in the big city on their own, taking turns to cook, buying

colourful stone nose-pins and walking on the busy streets. She was captivated by Salma's photos, shown on her recently acquired 'mobile'; great red-brick buildings with trees, like in the books, with Salma wearing shiny black glasses.

Yes, Shewli did want to work one day, but not yet. If she passed her exams, she could get a better job. Thankfully her mother quietly but firmly insisted that her daughter's education continue. Her *Mama*, with whom the final decision lay, relented on the basis of his childhood affection for her mother. Shewli knew she would make a better life for herself when the time came. Her good mathematics results, despite it being a 'boys' subject', proved she could do what she set her mind to.

Shewli did what she was told, keeping her dreams to herself. That is, until she met *him*. He was older than her, a friend of her cousin Hassan. She had never really noticed him until she started her water collection routine. His family was well known in the area. He came regularly to the nearby *basher jhar*, the bamboo grove, where he supervised the workers cutting branches. She had to walk past the green kaleidoscope of shades and the cooling breezes of the grove to collect water from the community tubewell, now that theirs had been deemed unfit because of arsenic contamination.

She usually made about four trips with the heavy pot, the *matir kolshi*, that others appeared to carry so gracefully. Water was forever slopping, as she shifted its weight from one hip to another. While passing the impermanent teashop, she furtively tried to overhear conversations. Frustrated that the women yapped on about village gossip, fake jewellery or the latest *Keya* or *Fair & Lovely* cream, it intrigued her to know what men talked about, though she suspected it wasn't as important as they made out.

She had often seen *him* from afar. He was taller than the rest, and looked animated while chatting with the others, drawing them in. She was charmed by the way he lit up his *beedi*, confidently, pausing before taking a puff. He looked like one of the film 'heroes', whose faces she had cut out from a newspaper *thonga* bag once and stuck on the inside of her *almirah* door. She loved the way his hair flopped over his face, and the casual way he commanded the attention of even those much older. She had heard he was good at his studies, unlike the shiftless lads that played cards all day. He was ambitious. He wanted more out of life—just like her.

She soon had the encounter for which she had secretly been hoping. She was in a rush that day, late with her chores. Running back from the pump, she slipped on the loose soil at the side of the path and fell. When she looked up he was standing over her.

'Did you hurt yourself?' he asked, looking into her eyes. Embarrassed, she just shook her head.

'Here,' he volunteered, extending a hand. Not wanting to appear helpless, she fought back the pain she suddenly felt in her ankle and sprang up, wincing. He noticed she was struggling, 'I'll get that,' he said, quickly picking up the water pot. Her clothes were smeared with sticky red mud. She must look a mess, she thought, mortified.

'Shall we go and fill it up?' he asked, still hanging on to the container.

'It's okay, I can do it. Shouldn't have been so careless,' she retorted quickly, not wanting to appear as foolish as she felt. She grabbed it from him. Then, feeling she had reacted too strongly, softened, 'My name is Shewli.' She was being too 'forward', but she couldn't think of anything else to say.

'Yes, you're Hassan's cousin. My name is Selim. I see you walking every morning. I don't know how you do it. Water *kolshis* are so heavy.' He gave her a dazzling smile and pretended to lift an imaginary jug and then collapse from the weight of it. She laughed back, despite herself. He looked even better up close. The nearness of him made her heart pound. She was almost afraid that he could hear. She couldn't believe that he had noticed her.

'I'd better be off, it's getting late. See you,' she said hurriedly, nearly tripping again in her haste to hide the deep blush that spread over her face.

Shewli spent the rest of the day in a daze, hardly listening to the schoolteacher and barely aware of what was going on around her. When she thought of their meeting she felt a quiver inside. She couldn't wait to go to the tubewell again.

It was the next morning, and there he was just leaving the tea stall. He caught her eye, and winked. Shewli felt a thrill within her, quickly looking away lest anyone else notice.

It became a routine. She hurried to get her chores done in anticipation of seeing him, often bumping into him as he emerged from the bamboo grove. She was charged with emotion; feeling light-headed one minute, impatient to see him the next. Somehow, since meeting him, she felt even more compelled to excel at her studies. His zest for life reinforced her own ambitions.

Preparation for the exam was still a scary prospect though, given she didn't have the private tutor that the more affluent students had. Surprising everyone by winning the coveted school *britti* scholarship had instilled an inner confidence in her. She would study late, by the light of a hurricane lamp, going through reams of *dista* paper. Her *Mama* complained to her mother that none of his children had gone through so much paper. They were simply not as serious as her Shewli, her mother proudly explained.

Sakina, her *Mama*'s younger daughter, was her confidante; 'Sakina, he's just so smart. We talk about everything. He knows so much. The other day he was explaining the elections to me. You know, he actually listens to me. Doesn't put me down just because I'm a woman. And when he looks at me with those deep eyes....'

'What? What?" her cousin would ask excitedly. This was so much like the love stories they heard about; but better, because it was real.

'When I'm with him I feel I can do anything.'

"Shewli, you're intelligent too. I wouldn't even understand all that stuff. He's also so *bhodro*, a real gentleman. Everyone says so,' her cousin added encouragingly, while they sat whispering on Shewli's bed, munching freshly plucked sour *bilumboo* fruit, with ground red chilli and salt.

The cousins would talk late into the night, and at other times Shewli daydreamed about him. One day as she was having a quick exchange with him amongst the branches, Selim picked up one of her earrings which had fallen off, and stooped to put it back in her ear, moving her hair to one side. The sensation of his hand on her neck was electric, and she knew right away that all she wanted was for him to touch her again. At that moment, the bamboo cutters trooped back from their tea break, interrupting them.

They stole moments together. With so many prying eyes, it was difficult. She started going to the well in the afternoons and immediately noticed that he was there. So after lunch, she would insist on going to fetch water again. They could then have some time together; the bamboo cutters worked deep inside the grove, and there was no one else in sight.

'You have that determined look,' he would say, 'I like that in a girl. You know what you want. You don't giggle like the others. Yet you have the sweetest smile.' He liked the way she listened to him, he said, with such concentration. She loved the way that they could banter back and forth. Or just sit in silence, as he carved out shapes in the bamboo while she looked on. He would discuss his frustrations regarding his brothers, and his dream of doing better for himself.

'I sometimes imagine us living in Dhaka, like those couples on TV,' she confided to Sakina. Currently he was looking after some family land, in exchange for an education. Apprenticing as a mechanic, he wanted to be a diploma engineer. He hoped to go abroad, or work in one of the big companies in Dhaka.

She herself found the prospect of village life constricting. Salma had recently got a better job in another factory, which didn't hold back overtime payments, and where she was now on an important committee. Salma talked of shopping for 'three piece' *shalwar kameez* sets on her days off, and going to the cinema. No one cared about your family background, whether you were married or not. Only how many collars you could make in an hour. Shewli was sure she could be good at that. She didn't want a future hemmed in by the opinion of others.

At the same time, she was becoming more and more attached to Selim. Her growing feelings came with an emerging urge for something she could not quite comprehend, which was both exhilarating and frightening. The more time they spent alone, the more she was caught in its vortex.

It happened one afternoon, when they met at a banana tree grove, with no one else around. She had sensed his need for her. His looks were more intense, his touch more lingering. He was always proper, even when she inwardly begged him not to be. His hand on the small of her back as they walked made her want to ask him to hold her. When he kissed her, she felt an incredible rush in her head, along with an unfamiliar stirring. The exquisite sweetness of it was something she replayed in her mind a thousand times later—lying in bed listening to the racket of frogs at night, or while helping her mother as she cooked the evening meal. The kiss made her feel like she was floating on air, cocooned in a bubble.

She had been seeing him for over ten months, their bond showing no sign of dissipating. 'When we're not together I think about him all the time,' Shewli told Sakina. She kept silent however, about her increasingly intense physical reactions. When he touched her one day, tracing her lips and chin, she felt a tingling, which shot through her body, her breasts drawing taut against her *kameez*. She was filled with a latent longing, which exposed something deep in her. She didn't want to get distracted from her exams, but she couldn't help it.

They usually met a few times each week. Even a look from him was enough to make her feel a throbbing in her groin. 'I'll stop if you want, just tell me to,' he said many times. She did, and then pulled him back to her, never wanting to let him go. When Shewli was hesitant, he drew her close, saying he had never felt this way before. Her body responded to his. Her hands explored him as if they had a will of their own. And then one day he was inside her, and they were making love before she had fully understood what was happening. She felt an indescribable array of sensations, cradled in his arms.

Just before her exams, she became increasingly irritable, and began to throw up. 'Shewli always feels tension before her exams,' her mother explained, as her bouts of nausea didn't lessen. She felt strange on the first day of her exams, as if her mind wasn't her own. Somehow she still managed to answer all the questions.

She didn't have time during the exam period to go to the doctor, which was a long drawn out affair; spending hours sitting on plastic pharmacy seats with hundreds of people around, until the time finally came when someone would shove a thermometer down her throat, and write an incomprehensible list of medicines. Her cousin, with whom she was sent, would invariably just choose one or two at his discretion.

Her brain couldn't process anything. Perhaps it was because she had decided to see less of him because of her exams. She missed him with an aching she couldn't describe, was nervous about the exams and just felt generally out of sorts. When she started to feel something hard in her stomach, she feared it was a tumour like the one her *Nani* had died of. They waited till her exams were over.

Finally taken by her *Mama* to the district hospital, she was frightened. She had managed to meet Selim the day before, in an abandoned cow hut, which had old dung, scattered everywhere. It didn't matter; it was just blissful to be in the comfort of his arms. She was terrified that she could not be cured. She melodramatically envisaged their love would end by her dying of an incurable disease with him heartbroken, like a cheesy film.

When she first heard what the doctor said as he put some instrument on her stomach while looking at the screen, she was almost paralyzed with shock. 'This girl has a baby in her tummy.' She kept hearing the words reverberating in her mind, drowning out the surrounding commotion. 'This girl has a baby in her tummy.' 'A baby.'

After that her life changed. Her mother shouted at her, hitting her repeatedly and demanding to know who had taken her innocence.

'I love him, *Ma*' she kept saying in her soul. Not aloud, though. Not until she had talked to him.

'Who did this, you must tell me!' her mother implored as her eyes both begged and berated her.

'It was Selim,' she whispered. 'But he didn't make me do anything.'

'What is she saying?' her mother looked enquiringly at Hasina *Apu*, Sakina's older sister, with incomprehension in her eyes.

Nasima *Mami* unleashed a screaming tirade at her husband, demanding that his sister and her family be put out of their house, having brought shame on the entire family. 'Huh, little *mem shaheb*, the perfect student, is not so perfect, is she? Turns out she has behaved worse than a street girl! I knew they would bring trouble to us, but do you ever listen to me? No!' Shewli's *Mami* ranted on to her subdued *Mama*.

While being 'a good studious girl' had helped their precarious position in the household, this situation exposed them to a raw vulnerability. Neighbours spat at her, and shouted out, '*Khanki*, whore.' The words hit her like stones.

She had to see him.

They had previously arranged to meet the following day near the pump. She was at first impatient when he was late, and then frantic, knowing that she would be missed if she didn't get back soon. Soon after, she was stopped from going out to collect water. She finally managed to sneak out to the grove a couple of days later, but saw no sign of him. She reluctantly approached Hassan, 'Can you give him a message? I have to see him.'

Hassan *Bhai*, who had always been so warm and loving, looked at her with a mixture of contempt, and an expression she couldn't quite place, which made her feel uncomfortable. He told her, in no uncertain terms, how she had disgraced the family.

Hasina *Apu* came up to talk to her again, 'Why don't you tell the truth? Selim took your honour; to what decent girl would this happen? You need to get married right away. Otherwise *Baba* and *Ma* will have no choice but to turn you all out. You have to think of all of us. You know, Selim denies that he raped you.'

'He didn't rape me,' she said, crying to Sakina, as they had a secret chat by the pond while they washed clothes, Nasima *Mami* having banned Sakina from talking to her. 'I just want to see him, Saki.'

'But how did this baby thing happen then?' Sakina asked bewildered, 'How come you are having a baby?'

'It just seemed so right. I didn't know anything like this would happen. I don't want to get married. Maybe one day, but not now. What will happen to my studies? You know all the married women around here, Saki. I never wanted to end up like them. It's like there is a chain tying me down,' she wailed to her cousin. At the same time she still longed to see him, thinking of their times together, his gentle teasing, his tenderness and their surreptitious embraces. Why wasn't he contacting her?

'Shewli, what will you do? *Ma* says none of us will be able to get married. You have no choice. Anyway, he is crazy about you. Being married to him will be different.'

'I know, but I still feel suffocated. I just need to talk to him. Nothing feels good right now. I can't understand why he is not turning up to any of our usual places. None of my messages seem to be reaching him,' she replied, trying to hide the desperation in her voice. 'I also can't believe that there is something living in me,' she added.

What was difficult to comprehend was that this thing inside her brought with it such a heavy burden of stigma, one that threatened to destroy her life. It wasn't just the 'dishonour'; it was the fact her future was being snatched away. She deeply resented the entity inside her, even as she felt outraged that she and her baby were tainted by shame.

About a week later, her *Mama* returned from a meeting with the elders. He slumped down, suddenly looking old. She felt a pang of guilt, as she peeked through the doorway with her head covered, listening to him report back. How could something so beautiful now appear so crude and ugly? It was official; Selim had denied that he was the father of Shewli's child. He acknowledged that he may have talked to her, but the child's father was obviously someone else.

Her first reaction was utter disbelief. She had to try Hassan again, even though he was behaving oddly with her, and had started making snide remarks, 'Hassan *Bhai*, please, I need to see him. I'm going mad.' All she wanted was to see those piercing eyes gazing into hers. To forget reality for a few minutes before the nightmare began again. She could just picture it, all the gossip spreading around like wildfire.

Selim wouldn't agree to a meeting. The next time she saw him was at the gathering of *Murubbis;* the elders were trying to work out a solution to 'the situation'. Opinions were catapulted around. She listened as others described her. The letch of a doctor, with others, speculated as to who had 'enjoyed' spending time with her. They seemed excited by the interrogation.

She kept silent, but felt like she was dying when she looked in his direction. He didn't acknowledge her, and those warm loving eyes had turned stone cold and distant. Then she heard it all too clearly; his denial. He could not possibly be the father. It must be someone else. But who could it be? 'I often saw her talking to the hired help at the bamboo grove,' was what he said.

She was stunned. 'Yes,' she felt like screaming, 'when I was waiting for you!'

She realized there would be no resurrection from this prison trap. The Selim she knew had disappeared, or had never been. The magnitude of what was happening began to dawn on her. Their special moments were a distant blur. Those haunting eyes had locked her out. They were no longer probing, joking, flirting, loving or wooing her.

Shewli wasn't sure what was worse, the reality of his metamorphosis, or the dreadful predicament in which she found herself. She felt she was falling down a bottomless pit. She wanted to reach out and grasp on to the disintegrating sides. She felt denigrated to the level of the tawdry sex workers who congregated near the slum shanties of the district town. His inexplicable betrayal cut through her like a knife.

She refused to say anything, so the elders ruled that she had been 'loose' with one of the hired hands. With such a bright future, why would Selim waste his life on someone like her?

The person who she had trusted the most had turned on her, in the cruellest way. She was still reeling from it. She found out later that his family had got to him. They told him he could either choose her and forfeit their support, or deny his involvement with her. He chose the easy way out.

The arguments at home continued. Recriminations were relentless. Every night there were screaming fights between *Mama* and *Mami*, where her *Mama* would refuse to throw his only sister out. Shewli didn't know how to deal with it, banging her head silently on her pillow. Selim's disengagement was still so raw.

To clear her head one afternoon, she went to the pond, surrounded by *badam* and *narikel* trees at the back, where the women bathed. As she felt the cool green-brown soothing water over her, she tried to hold onto every bit of sanity she had. Each dip refreshed her as she realized she just needed to believe in herself. When dusk descended, she reluctantly emerged from the water, her hair dripping. She was hurrying back to her room with her damp sari clinging to her, through the dense *shupari* tree plantation, when she ran into Hassan *Bhai*. He had a weird expression on his face, as he blocked her.'Where are you going in such a rush, Shewli?' he asked in a strange tone that did not sound like the Hassan *Bhai* she knew.

'Hassan *Bhai*, I'm going to change. Just taken a bath, you can see I'm wet,' she said, lightly, a bit out of breath.

'What's the hurry? We have been so close always. Why don't you show me how close you can be? You seemed to have no problem showing him,' he said with a suggestive smirk.

Shewli couldn't believe what she was witnessing. She felt sick to her stomach, her beloved Hassan *Bhai* turning into someone unrecognizable before her. She looked up at him, with a mixture of disgust, hurt and defiance, 'Leave me alone—you should be ashamed of yourself. Now let me go and change,' she retorted as she shoved him out of her way before running to her hut.

She began to understand why other girls took poison or hanged themselves from ceiling fans. Not that she was about to do any of those things, but the pain and humiliation were overwhelming. Selim was not by her side. She was a target for unwanted attention; she could feel the overt leers of the village men mentally stripping her. Young boys jeered at Shewli, making obscene gestures, while others turned their heads as they walked past. She had shown Selim a good time; why couldn't she show them some?

She felt the judgmental eyes of the elders. She had also managed to keep Hassan *Bhai*'s unwanted advances at bay, but she wasn't sure for how long. He was becoming more persistent and difficult to avoid. She was fair game. Her lost innocence was an open invitation to others who thought she was now no better than a whore. She just had to believe she would survive, but she still found unconscious tears dripping down her face.

Her body was slowly becoming attuned to the life growing

in her. Getting rid of it was on everyone's mind. The doctor had told them it was too dangerous. The baby was too big now. Her *Mama* had even offered to pay him extra to do it unofficially. The doctor didn't give in to this lucrative offer. Not that he was suddenly stricken by a conscience; he was being evaluated by some NGO group helping with a government project. Shewli had no choice but to go through with the birth.

Her mother was also adamant in her refusal to take Shewli to the woman who could give her special herbs, and use a wire to get rid of the 'mess' she was in. One of her cousins had died after such an incident many years ago, and it remained etched in the family memory. She would not risk her daughter's life, whatever the circumstances. No, all that needed to be done, her mother decided, was to get Shewli married quickly. It had to be to Selim—who else would marry her? He needed to take responsibility for what he had done. 'All I wanted was to get rid of this thing inside me. Life would be much simpler. But now, a part of me feels relieved that I have to keep it,' Shewli confided to Sakina, during another clandestine chat.

Shewli was overwhelmed with confusing and distressing emotions; a simmering rage against Selim, indignation at the ignominious insults she constantly faced, the awareness that there was something precious inside her alongside a great fear of losing the life of which she had dreamed, having it slip away as she was locked into a lifetime of domestic servitude.

Her mother was determined, once she put her mind to it. She was now on a mission to get Selim to marry her daughter. There was a local women's group, *Shakti,* which helped women who had suffered violence from their husbands. '*Shakti* is well known to those higher up,' her mother said.

'It's pointless,' her *Mama* told her mother flatly, 'Selim's family is so influential; his uncle is a Union Parishad member, his father is an authority on religious matters and his brothers are rich landlords. How can we take them on?'

However, her mother continued to try to convince the women to help. Every day she would put on an elaborate weeping performance to catch *Shakti's* attention. Yes, every day. Her diatribe varied little, 'Selim raped this young, simple girl, my only daughter. He denies he is the father. Her life is over. We will be homeless. The rich get away with everything; there is no justice for us poor. Only you women can help us.'

At first Shewli protested under her breath, embarrassed and troubled by her mother's routine, 'But *Ma*, it wasn't like that,' she muttered.

'What, how come a decent girl like you is in a situation like this? He knew what he was doing, all right. Tell me this, why is he not marrying you?'

After awhile it seemed futile to say anything. Nobody seemed to understand. Shewli felt so alone. Her tummy was prodded, her face held and examined, as she endured the hushed sympathy of some and hidden voyeurism from others. The constant sexual innuendos and harassment were an on-going hazard. The only way she could cope was by closing her mind to what was going on. As she lay on her cotton *godi* bed taking her afternoon rest, looking up at the straw woven *chon* patterns above her, she delved deep within to find the strength to go on.

Some days were just too much for her. 'I'm being paraded

about like a doll, everyone looking at me with that disdainful superiority. Worst are those well-meaning *Khalas* who are so patronizing! It's unbearable, yet I have to will myself to keep quiet. I pretend I'm somewhere else. Whatever anyone says about it being Selim's fault, I can see in the look in their eyes,' she vented to her cousin at the end of one exhausting day.

'What can you do? I feel like killing him too, the bastard. Can't believe he left you to face all this. Doesn't he have any decency?' Sakina sympathized, fuming.

'We did have something. I still believe that,' Shewli tried to reason with herself, even as she felt unable to contain her anger, as if it would explode any moment.

Selim's family heard about their visits to *Shakti*. His brothers convinced the local chairman to tell them to back off. 'Then ask him to marry Shewli,' her *Mama* simply said. The local hoodlums then beat up Hassan. Nasima *Mami* also tried to get Shewli's mother to accept the meagre amount of money that his family offered to settle the 'matter'. 'We are all being further disgraced by you going around like this,' she derided.

'This means that we have some power now, otherwise why would they threaten us?' her mother calmly responded, refusing to give in. Shewli wasn't sure how she felt anymore. The whole village seemed against them, yet there was this life blossoming within her. Didn't Selim feel an ounce of responsibility? How could she have fallen for someone so spineless? She shuddered at her gullibility. He had forsaken his own; what kind of a man was he? She started feeling protective towards her unborn child, sitting for hours in the papaya garden at the back of their settlement feeling her baby kick.

Shewli was so big now she could hardly move, but she still had to be on show. Often they had to wait outside houses. Unperturbed, her mother would sit with her on the side of the dirt road, like a common beggar, and loudly bemoan the predicament of her daughter for all to hear.

For a time it was all Shewli could do to stop lashing out at Selim. There were moments when she had thought about revenge. However Shewli's anger had begun to ebb. Her energy was redirected into a consuming need to get her life back under control.

The sequence of events initiated by her mother started gaining momentum. A kind looking woman approached her, 'Shewli, do you want to tell me, just me, what happened?'

'No, he didn't,' she responded when gently questioned if Selim had threatened her.

'Did you think that he would marry you?' she quietly asked.

'I thought we would get married one day, sure.'

'Was there any other boy who you have been close as you have with Selim?' the older woman asked softly.

'No!' Shewli found herself raising her voice.

Shakti did decide to help them. Just after, Shewli gave birth to a beautiful baby girl. When she held her daughter in her arms, the young woman felt peace and wonderment, despite the furore raging around them. Shewli couldn't figure out how an innocent being could be treated like a monster just because her father wouldn't acknowledge her.

There was talk of bringing a rape charge against Selim; he would be put in jail straight away, which would give them a strong negotiating position to make him reconsider marriage, the only way of protecting Shewli and her child now.

The woman who had talked to Shewli spoke up, 'Selim's family want Shewli out of their lives by paying her a pittance. What will happen to this poor child? Without her father's name she will be no one. Maybe we should file a case of seduction. He is denying paternity and defaming her character,' she reasoned, 'unless we use the law to force their hand, he will not admit to being the father. However, he didn't actually force her.'

Rallies and procession *micheels* were held. *Shakti* lobbied the District Commissioner's Office, the police, and the media. They involved people in the community.

Selim's family still only offered money; they were not prepared for 'that slut' to be married into their family. The worrying development however was that word was out that the court was about to acquit Selim, due to the lack of evidence. Shewli was amazed at her mother's tenacity to just not give up.

Then, one day, there was great excitement. A new medical test, called *Dee En Ay*, could prove that Selim was the father. This test had recently been made available in Dhaka Medical. *Shakti* managed to get some local businessmen to fund it. The final result was announced with pomp and ceremony, Selim being declared as the father of Shewli's daughter. Shewli, on hearing the news, not only felt vindicated but also had a sense of closure, knowing that her daughter's position was secure. Selim's family was told that they had better agree quickly to a marriage.

One foggy winter morning, Selim was brought to a shack, which his uncle had reluctantly rented at a reduced rate to the newlyweds. Selim's father had refused to give the couple a home. So much had happened that Shewli had not had the time to absorb it all. 'It's like a drama. I have nothing to say to Selim. But I need to do this,' Shewli shared with Sakina as her mother got her ready for the marriage ceremony, putting on a pair of gold earrings which had been her own wedding *jhumkas*.

'I know he wasn't there for you, but he was under a lot of pressure from his family. Maybe he really does love you. Will you forgive him, then?' her cousin asked, trying to ascertain Shewli's state of mind.

'Saki, he is the father of my child; a child that came out of our love. Whatever anyone says, I know it was special. Now, as Selim's daughter, she has a place in this world. As for what I feel now about him, it's way beyond whether I forgive him or not. I am just a different person now. I am doing what I have to do,' Shewli dryly stated.

A hurried *Akht* had been arranged with the local Imam, who was 'in form', morally lecturing away. The birth of her daughter was registered, rescinding her illegitimate status. The *Kabeen Nama*, the marriage contract, was signed with witnesses from *Shakti*. A price of 50,000 *taka* was fixed as the *Den mohor*. Shewli knew she was supposed to get that money if the marriage did not work out. She looked at Selim as he stared vacantly ahead, the person with whom she had been so intimate, the father of her child. It didn't matter anymore.

They both sat woodenly, with noise and activity all around them. She looked around at this surreal set up, and took a deep breath. It was as if she was drifting above, looking down; Selim's expressionless face, her rigid body, the baby's softness, her mother's resilience, the righteous *Shakti* women and the important men patting themselves on the back, basking in praise for being on the side of justice.

Her exam results had come in before her daughter was born. She had butterflies while she anxiously waited for them. This time she had gone by herself; no Hassan *Bhai* to help her. No one else was bothered, any good news being subservient to the pervasive scandal. As she strained to see the piece of paper stuck on the college notice board through the hordes of other clamouring students, she found out she had achieved one of the highest marks in the district.

Shewli remembered her results, and felt a tempered optimism. She sensed the promise of a new beginning. She knew they, she and her baby, would somehow make it. She held her little one tight. Now they had a ticket to something better.

She would contact Salma about a job. The *Shakti* women could help, she was sure. She recalled them talking about day-care. She smiled inside, closed her eyes, and as she listened to the Imam's *munajat* blessing them, she started to daydream.

Be

ALIZEH AHMED

I glance around nervously, noticing how beautiful everyone looks. The music is loud, the beat shaking its way through every cell of my body, making my tissues vibrate. Voiceless chatter fills up the nooks and corners of the bar, stifling my sense of security. Everyone seems to be rapt in serious conversation or engaged in flirtatious banter—that is, until I step into the room, friendless.

All eyes turn my way. Through the smoke, they look me up and down. The women are judgmental. Harsh. They think I look cheap and skanky. Hostile looks sear my skin, leaving me feeling naked. The men undress me with their eyes.

My knees feel shaky. I shouldn't have come. I turn around to flee this cage.

And then, all of a sudden...

my left shoulder jerks up.

And then my right.

It's almost as though—OH NO!

My left knee.

How embarrassing!

My entire body is twisting into weird positions.

Suddenly, I feel my head leaning backwards in slow motion, and I inhale deeply.

And before I can stop myself, I belt out

'LET'S DO THE TWIST!!!'

I can't stop shaking my body to the classic rhythms of Chubby Checker!

I'm on the dance floor, all by myself, everyone watching me—but I just love this song too much to stop.

One by one, people start hopping onto the wooden floor, giving me a shy nod, and so I wave back, as my body convulses to the beat.

And then, I realise: I can push all of these worrisome voices out of my head—

and just...

BE!!!

About the Editor

Farah Ghuznavi is a writer, translator and newspaper columnist, with a background in development work. She holds an undergraduate and two postgraduate degrees from the London School of Economics, and has worked for the Grameen Bank and the United Nations Development Programme, as well as NGOs in the UK, Bangladesh and elsewhere. She remains an unrepentant idealist despite the existence of empirical evidence suggesting that it might be better to think otherwise.

Farah began writing fiction in a desperate attempt to make the stories leave her in peace, in the hope that putting them down on paper would send them on their way. So far, this strategy appears to be working, one story at a time. Farah's work has been published in a number of story collections and literary magazines in Britain, the US, Canada, Singapore and her native Bangladesh. These include the fiction anthologies *The Storm is Coming* (Sleeping Cat Books, USA), *Curbside Splendor Issues 1 and 2* (Curbside Splendor, USA), *The Path, Winter Issue 2011* (The Path to Publication, USA) and *Woman's Work* (Girl Child Press, USA); *Lady Fest: Winning Stories from the Oxford Gender Equality Festival* (Dead Ink, UK), *The*

Monster Book for Girls (Exaggerated Press, UK) and *Journeys* (Sampad, UK); *The Rainbow Feast* (Marshall Cavendish, Singapore); *What the Ink?* (Writer's Block, Bangladesh), *Sticks and Stones Vol. 1* (Sticks and Stones, Bangladesh) and *From the Delta* (UPL, Bangladesh).

Her story "Judgement Day" was Highly Commended in the 2010 Commonwealth Short Story Competition, and another story, "Getting There", placed second in the Oxford Gender Equality Festival Short Story Competition. Farah has been working to finalise a manuscript of her own short stories alongside editing this anthology of new writing from Bangladesh for Zubaan. She is a regular contributor to *The Star Magazine*, which is affiliated to the *Daily Star* newspaper in Bangladesh, and writes a fortnightly column entitled "Food for Thought". Her website is under construction at: www.farahghuznavi.com

Contributors

Sabrina Fatma Ahmad was born and raised in Dhaka, Bangladesh, but currently resides in British Columbia, Canada. She has a BSS in Media and Communication from the Independent University, Bangladesh, and an MFA in Creative Writing. In addition to her columns and articles for the *Daily Star*, where she has been a feature writer for the past ten years, her work has been published by the British Council in Dhaka, Guildhall Press in Ireland, and Sampad South Asian Arts in the UK. Sabrina mostly writes prose, and specializes in short stories and microfiction.

Alizeh Ahmed did her undergraduate degree at Brown University, USA and her postgraduate in Public Health at the London School of Hygiene and Tropical Medicine, UK. She loves to read, travel and dance.

Sharbari Ahmed received her MA in Creative Writing, Fiction from New York University. Her stories have appeared in *The Gettysburg Review, The Caravan, The Asian Pacific American Journal, Salt, Catamaran and the Zine, Ripe Guava,* and in the anthology *A New Anthem* (Tranquebar, India, 2009). She is also a playwright. Her first play "Raisins Not Virgins" was produced in NYC, LA, Boston, and Dhaka. She writes a column for *The Star Magazine* in Bangladesh and teaches writing and literature at Norwalk Community College, Connecticut. One of her greatest fears is that she will be deemed talented only after her death.

Srabonti Narmeen Ali has a B.A degree in Political Science and an M.A in Media and Communications. She is a staff writer for the *Daily Star* newspaper and the weekly magazine, *The Star*. During her free time she also tries to nurture her two other passions, singing and dancing. She was trained in Rabindra Sangeet (although she prefers singing in English) and also took Kathak lessons when she was younger. She is currently living in Dhaka with her husband and son.

S. Bari lives and works in Switzerland.

Abeer Hoque is a Nigerian born Bangladeshi American writer and photographer. "Wax Doll" is an excerpt from her novel in stories, *The Lovers and the Leavers*. See more at www.olivewitch.com

Lori S. Khan resides in Dhaka with her husband and three children where she spends her time running her own catering company, and is part of a writing collective known as Writer's Block. Lori is a poet who has recently begun experimenting with short fiction and plays. Her work has been published in a number of magazines and supplements in Bangladesh, and also features in the anthology *What the Ink?* recently published by Writer's Block.

Rubaiyat Khan was born in Dhaka, Bangladesh. She completed her Bachelors in English Literature from Knox College, Illinois in 2002, followed by a Post-Baccalaureate tenure from the same, in Creative Writing and Theatre. She also completed her Masters in Fine Arts in Creative Writing in the genre of Fiction from The New School, NY, in 2009. She is currently an Adjunct Professor of English, and is scheduled to join the New Jersey Institute of Technology in Newark, NJ, from Fall 2012. Rubaiyat currently resides in a sunny suburb in New Jersey with her husband, and an incredibly spoiled gray Maine Coon cat named Bholanath Maximillian Kabir.

Munize Manzur lives in Dhaka, Bangladesh. She got her B.A. in English Literature from Bryn Mawr College, Pennsylvania, USA and M.A in Communications from Temple University, Pennsylvania, USA. Munize's short stories have been published in several anthologies (*From the Delta*: University Press Ltd, 2005. *Deshi Dreams*: Wayward Bride Press, 2007. *A Rainbow Feast*: Marshall Cavendish, 2010. *Journeys*: Sampad, 2010 & 2012), national newspapers (*Daily Star, New Age*), and international literary journals (*La Bouche, The Del Sol Review, Writers Hub*). Born to multi-task, Munize is currently looking to publish her collection of short stories while working on her first novel.

Tisa Muhaddes aspires to unveil the lives of people that are often marginalized and invisible within society. Her stories are inspired by the people she has encountered living in Brussels, Dhaka, New York and London. She has been published in a variety of literary magazines in Bangladesh, in an anthology of Bangladesh writers titled *What the Ink?*

and in a collection entitled *Journeys* by Sampad UK. She also has a column titled 'Sense and Sensibility' in the *Independent* weekly magazine in Bangladesh. She is currently working on a novel on sex workers. She resides in London.

Shabnam Nadiya grew up in Jahangirnagar, a small college campus in Bangladesh. She is a recent graduate and recipient of a Truman Capote Fellowship, and a Teaching Writing Fellowship at the MFA program at the Iowa Writers' Workshop; and is currently working on a collection of linked stories called *Pariah Dog and Other Stories*.

Iffat Nawaz is a Bangladeshi-American working and living in both countries, thriving for new experiences and insights. Her writing career started in 2003 with her column for the *Daily Star* newspaper titled "Under a Different Sky." An international development practitioner by profession, Iffat is constantly torn between the balance of east and west, and the inspiration of old cities versus the vastness of nature. She hopes to neatly gather these opposite pulls into the novel she is writing, and that you will be there to read it when it hopefully takes a life of its own.

Shazia Omar is a social psychologist. She completed her undergraduate degree at Dartmouth and then worked for a year as an investment banker in Manhattan. After three years of traveling, visiting ashrams and learning yoga, she completed a Masters at LSE. Shazia is a member of Writers Block Bangladesh. She works for UkAid and teaches yogilates. Her debut novel, *Like a Diamond in the Sky*, was published by Zubaan/Penguin India in 2009.

Sadaf Saaz Siddiqi studied Molecular Cell Biology at the University of Cambridge, and lives in Dhaka with her husband where she runs a business and learns Indian classical singing. She is a women's rights activist, and works to promote South Asian performing arts and culture. Her poems have been published in national dailies and in the *Journeys* and *Inspired by Tagore* collections by Sampad, as well as the anthology *What the Ink?*. Her poetry was featured in the short film 'Duniya'. She is currently working on an anthology of poems, and has recently started writing short stories.

At the risk of starting something
as I finish. I want to close
by pointing toward the issues to which
emergence but drawing attention to
some issues BWE brings up.

Our analysis of 71 as case study:
nation & metaphor
— family & nat'lism

limitations toward comparison
w/ Bengali, as I suggest
but also Pakistan (71)
& as Alam envisions a transSt
question of influence
languid options world global

Ending notes behind